BRUH, MY STORY IS NO DIFFERENT THAN YOURS

MICHAEL E MARTIN JR.

Printed in the United States of America
First Printing 2019
First Edition 2019

10 9 8 7 6 5 4 3 2 1

Editor: Tricia Dean

BRUH, MY STORY IS NO DIFFERENT THAN YOURS

TABLE OF CONTENTS

CHAPTER 1
BACK IN THE DAY

My Pops found a girlfriend, when I was like six years old. He gave up on his wife, marriage and his kids. My mother was stuck raising me and my sister all by herself. She worked two jobs just to keep a roof over our heads, and food on the table. Those years were really hard on my mother, and I knew that she was hurt. We had a 1975 Chevy Nova that started whenever it wanted to. I remember the early mornings, when my mother would make me step on the gas pedal while she sprayed carb-cleaner in the carburetor. The heat didn't work and the windows were always foggy; we still survived.

My sister and I went to a catholic school in the early 80's. My mother worked in the cafeteria at the elementary school around the corner. Upon school dismissal, we had to walk across the street and around the corner to my mother's job. My mother would give us a snack, and make us do our homework while we waited for her to get off work.

When my mother was finished working we would go home. My sister and I had to do our chores before we could do anything else. I had to clean my room, make sure all off the clothes in my drawer were folded, sweep down the back stairs, and take everything out and then clean the cabinets. My sister had to do the kitchen, clean the bathroom, and iron our clothes for school the next day. When I was finished with all my chores, I would go outside and play.

I guess mom couldn't take the loneliness, because she didn't wait that long to get herself a boyfriend. In 1981, my dad had a baby on the way by Beverly. Beverly was the woman who broke up our happy home. My mother was also pregnant by her boyfriend Steve. Usually my mother was the only adult working in our house. Steve was left taking care of the house. It wasn't like he had anything else to do.

I was constantly in the doghouse with Steve. The only time that I was not in trouble was when my mother was home. If I was finished with my chores and I asked to go outside, I would have to ask Steve. Sometimes he would say, "yeah", but usually the answer was no. He always had something to say about everything that I did. Whenever I would tell him that my chores were done, he would say, "If I go and look, and the shit ain't done right, your ass is mine and then you're going to your room for the rest of the night."

I would double check it, but eventually as time progressed I knew he was going to find something wrong with it anyway, so I didn't work that hard at cleaning up anymore.

Why should I?

He would go and observe my work, and then look at me and say, "Get your ass upstairs and take all of your clothes off. I told you don't play wit me."

I would get mad, and stomp up the stairs to my room.

"Stomp one more time in here, and I'm going to give you something to stomp about."

I was a hardheaded and stubborn little boy who just rebelled at authority. At a young age, I had realized that life wasn't about limits, it was about living. I liked to do the things that I was forbidden to do rather than those things that I wasn't.

I became the class clown at my school, and that's what kept me getting ass whipping's daily. I didn't get into trouble because I wasn't doing my work in school. Actually, my grades were good and I wasn't even putting forth my best effort. I just loved to make people laugh. Laughter is what made me forget about all of the things that were going on in my life. I would make jokes and my friend's would laugh.

That gave me the reassurance that I wasn't a failure, and my dad's leaving wasn't my fault. The truth is, that I missed my father and I felt that I wasn't getting the love and the attention that I deserved.

I remember the days, when I would hear my friend's ringing the doorbell, asking if I could come outside to play. Usually, they would be told that I was on punishment. Most of the time I didn't really want to go outside.

Two months after I was born, my father bought a house for us, in a predominantly white neighborhood. One day, I would be playing fine with my neighbors, and then they would team up with each other, jump me and call me a nigger. Richard and Joey were the only two white boys on my street who stuck up for me. They would come out of nowhere and say if you got a problem with him, then you've got a problem with me. And then the beef was on.

The fighting between us went on throughout my early elementary years, when I attended Build Academy and Campus North. We would play, and then we would fight. It was during those times, that I hated my parents for buying that house. We were the second black family to purchase a home on Dunlop Street. But if you ask me we were the only ones. The other black family lived on the corner, and they were all real light-skinned. I was dark as midnight, so I caught wreck. I would tell my mom what I was going through, and that I hated living there, but what I was saying, was going in one ear and right out the other.

Because of my situation at home, I spent a lot of time on Winslow, over my grandparent's house. My father's parents loved me to death. I would go over there and get treated like a prince. I also had a lot of friends over there to play with. My parent's lived in the house next door, before I was born. That's actually where they made me.

Pops was probably sampling the goods one night after work, and the rest is history. Winslow was in the hood, and blacks were everywhere. I dared my racist neighbors to come around here and call me a nigger. They would have got it brung to them. Shawn and Johnny were two of my best friends who lived on Winslow. The three of us collected Hot-Wheels cars. We would make car trails in the grass, forts near the tree, and play from sun up to sun down. Whenever we weren't playing with our cars, we chased after the fast girls in the neighborhood trying to play Hide-N-Go-Get-it.

Since my parents separated, the only time that my sister and I would see our father was for school shopping and Christmas. I was starting to hate him more and more each day. It was like he had forgotten all about me. He would promise to come and get me one day, and I wouldn't be able to sleep until that day came. I would sit on the steps in the house and jump up at the sound of every car coming down the street, but he would never show. I missed out on a lot of sleep waiting for my father, and yet, the day for us to spend time together never came. He would always buy me something the next time that we met. I guess that was his way of saying that he's sorry for standing me up.

My visits with my dad got shorter and he was having another child, by another woman named Katherine. My mother had another son a few years earlier that she named Lil Steve. I often asked myself how could my parents continue to have children, when they weren't even spending time with the one that they already had; me. I remember the day that my father came to my rescue, when I had gotten into trouble at Campus North. After they kicked me out of school my father asked me if I wanted to come and live with him. I agreed, and I must admit; this was like one of my prayers being answered.

Two days after I had gotten kicked out of school, I moved in with my father and his girlfriend Cathy. Cathy was nice. She had a son that was a few years younger than me, but he and I got along fine. At the time, Cathy was pregnant with my fathers fourth child. I thought that since I was living with my father, our relationship would be better, but I think it got worse. We would sit on the couch, watching movies all day, and never say a word to each other. My father wasn't mean, he was just firm. It would have been safe to say that I was a little bit frightened by my father. He starred at you in a way that would make anyone to forget the question that they were going to ask. As much as I wanted to be around him, I just stayed out of his way. After I was expelled from Campus North, I attended school #71. It was right around the corner from my father's house. Everyone at 71 called me Little LL, cause I wore a pair of black LL Coo J Troops. I had a very cute girlfriend at the time, named Tajuanna. She was light-skinned with long pretty hair, and she wore these real big, but cute glasses. I would walk Tajuanna home from school everyday. We would also talk on the phone for hours. Tajuanna was real cool, and I really enjoyed the time that we spent together.

I only lived at my father's house for one year, and then I moved back in with my mother. That was during the summer, right after my sister Katrina was born. She was a pretty chocolate little thing that loved to smile. For my father, there was no denying her because she had the Martin trademark—our nose. When I moved back I first noticed that Dunlop St had changed a lot over the years. I had now become friends with all of my neighbors who use to call me names in the past. Through the years more blacks started moving into the neighborhood. I guess my former hateful neighbors finally realized that blacks weren't going anywhere.

During those years, I had two close friends, who lived a few blocks from my mother's house. Jay and Jamil both went to Campus North. The principle at Campus North gave me a second chance, and I was happy to be attending Campus North with all of my old friends again. Jamil and I would to go to parties and walk to school together. Jay was into basketball, boxing and weightlifting, and Jamil was into dirt bikes and video games. They had a cousin named Miya, who used to come over their house. Miya was nice looking, and she dressed real fly. I didn't sweat her too tough back then though. I knew I would have her eventually; I just had to get my shit together. Jamil and I stayed the night over each other's house. We would talk about everything. I liked it when they would talk about their father, and how crazy he was. Their father's name was Julius, and they would always tell me stories about how he had a terrible attitude. Julius and my dad came from the same neighborhood and they played basketball together when they were kids.

One of the funniest stories that they ever told me was the one when they were living in the fruit belt on Grape St. They said that there was this car that kept speeding down their one-way street in the wrong direction. Their father came outside and yelled at the guy.

Then the guy got out the car, and told Julius that he could do whatever he wanted to do.

Julius punched him in the mouth hard as hell.

The man started talking stuff and then one of his friends got out the car. That's when Julius yelled upstairs and told his girlfriend Brenda to bring him his stick.

And then the guys just got in the car and pulled off. That story still cracks me up every time that I hear it.

CHAPTER 2
HIGH SCHOOL

In the fall of 1989, I attended Bennett High School. My freshman year was one of the best years of my life. Everybody from the hood went to Bennett. My mother worked at Bennett in the kitchen, and my big sister Michelle was a junior that year. Michelle was an "A" student who had received all kinds of rewards and accolades. My situation was a little different.

I thought that I was born to make people laugh. Everyone found me funny except my teachers and my principle Mrs. Whitman. Mrs. Whitman took her job just a little too serious. She came to Bennett to weed out the bad apples, and that's just what she did. She didn't waste any time suspending people. She had it in for me from day one. I lived in detention.

Whenever I wasn't in detention, I was usually running around the school trying to push up on anything that moved. There was this one girl name Toy, who was light-skinned, short and fly as hell. She was a junior. My freshman year, you couldn't tell me anything. I pressed my luck and went for all of the upper class women. I had a fetish for older women, and Toy was the perfect one to teach me a few things.

I also liked this one girl named Toya. Excuse me, I'm sorry, I mean a woman named Toya because that's just what she was. She was the flyest thing in Bennett that year. She would make a brotha wet his draws, just looking at her. She was real thick and she carried herself like a lady at all times. She used to rock Gucci gear like the shit was cheap. Everybody said that I had to have money to step to her, but while others was just watching, I was busy, trying my luck. I used to walk up to her and be like …

You need some of this young lovin in your life girl.

The response was always the same though.

"Little boy please."

That was nothing new though. Everyone called me little that year. I was only 5 ft 2 inches tall. My height didn't bother me though, I use to walk with my head up and my chest poked out like I was the shit. That year I even tried out for the football team. A few older guys tried to play me on my first day of school. That morning as I was walking down the hall on the second floor where everybody used to kick it at before classes started, a few of the upper class-men yelled, "Who let the little kids in?"

"Yo Mama did," I responded.

When I said that, he looked surprised. I guess he never expected a comeback like that from a freshman. I put him on Front Street in front of his crew. He cursed me and started chasing me.

That year, my sister was a cheerleader, and I already knew most of the football players from practice, so it was safe to say that I had juice at Bennett.

I was loving all of the attention that I was getting at Bennett, but that all came to a screeching halt, one day, while I was in swim class. I was just chillin in the shallow end of the pool, kicking it with my friend Tamika. Tamika was this young thick freak who liked me. When it came time for the class to end, she invited me into the girls locker-room to help her get dressed. I figured what the hell, and followed her into the dressing room. I was in there sitting down on the bench, while she started to get dressed. All of the other girls in the dressing room were just minding their own business.

Then this big head girl named Lulu got up and went to tell the teacher. I still can't figure out why she was buggin, it wasn't like someone was there for her. Lulu looked dead wrong, her hair was never done and she had the biggest buckteeth in the world. Lulu was the type of girl that if Stevie Wonder could see; he would wish he was still blind.

After that incident I was expelled. A few months later I was sent to live in California with my auntie Rita. Cali was real cool, the Spanish mami's that were out there made learning impossible. There was more variety when it came to women in Cali too. I used to talk to this one girl named Maria. Maria and her family had just moved to the U.S. from Mexico. She had hair down to her butt, thick beautiful lips, a nice booty and perfect hips. She made the rest of the women look like mud-ducks.

I had a few friends that I kicked it with. One girl that I was real cool with was Sharonda. Sharonda was seventeen years old, light skinned, tall and sexy. If you weren't in your late twenty's or early thirties, she wasn't hearing a thing that you had to say. I also had a friend named Percy. Percy was a boxer. I remember my first day of school, when I saw Percy beat up two people and knock out a third. Percy went with this girl named Felicia. Felicia was a dime piece for real. She had a brother named Kareem who worshiped the ground that

Michael Jordan walked on. Kareem loved basketball, and everyday, he had a different Michael Jordan t-shirt on.

Cali was very different than NY. When I went to school, I didn't have to be dressed like I was going to a fashion show everyday. In Cali they could care less about clothes. But in NY if you don't have any gear, you're like a hermit. I had another friend named Phillip. Phil was a playboy who had all the women. Phil's mother lived in Rialto, that's why he went to our school. But he spent most of his time in the Jordan Down Apartments in Watts, CA where his grandmother lived.

I didn't really do too much while I was in Cali. I was actually bored most of the time. As a result, in about seven months after I arrived in California, I went back home. When I went back home there was something very strange going on. My whole crew had white girlfriends. I later found out why Jungle Fever was so prominent within my crew. The white girls wouldn't argue or put up a fight like the sisters did. They did whatever they were told, and they spent all of mommy and daddy's money on their man. Not long after I had come home, my man Jamil hooked me up with this one chick named Megan. Megan was not one the finest white girls in the world, and she also had a little weight to her. But I could over look that cause Jamil told me from the start that she pays like she weigh. Megan had a sister named Vanessa who looked like Madonna. Everybody in the whole crew wanted to sleep with Vanessa, and she knew it. She dressed just like a hoe and I later found out that's just what she was. She wore a lot of make-up and she always had a little mini-skirt on.

On Friday's and Saturday's my crew went to this hip hop club in Amherst, NY called the Toy Store. After my first visit to the club, I immediately realized why all of my people's had white girlfriends; there was nothing but interracial couples in the whole club. One night I went there and met this girl named Nesha. Nesha was a black girl who had just moved to Buffalo, NY from Pittsburgh, PA. Nesha was too THICK. It looked like her parents just fed her ham hocks and cornbread, for breakfast, lunch and dinner. I was attracted to Nesha because she was not only cute, but she was also real sweet, and she knew how to dance. Nesha had a friend named Liz who was with her that night. Liz pushed up on my man Jay. That night we all had a ball. After that night and a few more conversations, I just had to have Nesha on my team.

I attended Buffalo Traditional during my junior year of high school. I went there, with my old crew from Build Academy elementary school. I had one girlfriend named

Kamala that I used to talk to while I was there. Kamala was like 5ft 2inches tall, dark-skinned, bowlegged and she had a fat booty. We used to talk the night away on the phone. I also had a friend named Michelle, who was on the Crusaders drill team. They won the competition almost every year. During my junior year, I was accepted and I graduated from the Mayor's Youth Leadership Program. I really enjoyed participating in the program. I met a lot of nice people. At most of our functions, I kicked it with my friends Ebony and Kidadah.

These were two of the darkest, and sexiest sisters I have ever met in my life. We use to tell jokes and bug out at every meeting. They made the time go by so much faster. I was later kicked out of Buffalo Traditional for treatening to punch a teacher in the mouth. After that incident I was sent to Buffalo Alternative. The schools name spoke for itself—no other alternative. Still I think I learned more at that school than most others that I had attended. The teachers there were genuine and they cared about their jobs, and their students. You could always talk to most of the teachers about anything. It was also at Buffalo Alternative that I was finally able to finish the computer game "Oregon Trail." After a few months I was able to go before the board and show them that

I was rehabilitated, and was able to go to a regular high school, and so, my wish was granted.

My senior year was off the hook. I went to Grover Cleveland High. I had a steady girlfriend during most of the year, named Liz. Liz was Puerto Rican and one of the thickest thangs in town. She was real sweet too. I was also talking to this sister named Myisha while I was going with her, but I had to let Myisha go after she gave up the butt to my man Derrick, I guess I was too slow for her.

That year I also had a job at this restaurant called Wurtzburger Hof that was around the corner from my house. There's a funny thing about my job there. At one time blacks weren't allowed to eat in the restaurant at all. Blacks had to pick up their food at the side door and take it home. I felt that I was breaking a barrier by becoming the second black to work for them. I literally lived at work. They had to pay me to take the day off. I loved working there and all the interesting people that I met made everyday a great experience. Especially Mel. Mel was a professor at the local community college, who used to talk to me about college and my goals in life—Mel was great.

During my senior year in the month of November, a terrible accident occurred, while I was using my snow blower.

As I was plowing the sidewalk with my snow blower a few houses down, from my mother's house. While I was coming back down the street to my house, my snow blower got clogged and stopped running.

As I bent down to pull the lever on my snow blower, so that I could put it in reverse. My hand got caught in the blades. My hand was going down further and further, and when I yanked my hand out there was blood everywhere. I then twisted my fingers back and forth, and I was able to see my bones; just like a skeleton. I picked up my skin and my fingernails off of the ground and ran back down the street to my house. I slipped as soon as I reached my driveway. Jamil was in the yard watering down the snow like it was flowers. He dropped the hose and rushed to my rescue. We went into the house and my little brother Steve called 911. The ambulance came about 10 minutes later and took me to the hospital. I was out of school for like three days.

When I returned to school everybody wanted to know what happened to me. Liz was real sweet through the whole ordeal. She treated her Papi like a King.

CHAPTER 3
RENEE

I met Renee, while I was working at Mike's. Mike's was a local restaurant on the same street as Wurtzburger Hof, just farther down, where a lot of people just hung out. The word was that Renee was a little hot in the pants. All the guys that worked at the restaurant wanted to talk to Renee. Most of them just wanted to hit it though.

Initially I would make comments and flirt with her. One evening while I was working, my man Jay told me that she liked me. After I heard that, it didn't take long for me to push up on her. Four week's after she had started to work at Mike's, we began to date each other.

In the beginning, I used to always feel like I was not the only one Renee was seeing.. And besides, girlfriend had a rep. She used to talk to madd brotha's that I knew. That bothered me because; I always felt that brotha's were laughing at me. When Renee and I would go out together, it was like I could hear their voices, and read the expressions on their faces.

"I hit that"

"Yeah me too."

You know how brotha's do.

It was those kind's of thought's which stuck in my head.

From the start of our relationship, I never gave Renee the benefit of the doubt. It seemed like the only good times that we shared were when we were alone. During those times we just focused on what we had at that particular moment, which was each other. Renee was really beautiful and smart as hell in school. Sometimes we would talk about her past, and the choices that she had made. Her mother, who was never around to supervise Renee's activities, was supposedly raising Renee. As a result of her mother's absence, Renee was basically raising herself. Initially I was like everyone else. I just wanted to hit it and quit it, but after spending more and more time with her, I felt that this was a woman that I could someday fall in love with.

I remember the first time that Renee and I had sex.

I went over Renee's house that evening at about 8:00PM. Her mother called the house right after I had come over. Once Renee hung up the phone with her she said

"My mother aint coming home tonight. You can spend the night if you want to."

I don't know because I have to take my mothers car home.

"Ok well, don't say that I didn't ask,"

We popped a movie in the VCR and cuddled on her mother's white leather sofa. I sat in the corner, leaning to the side, trying to be cool you know? She positioned herself on me. Her head was resting comfortably on my chest, while both of our legs were intertwined.

I had a very beautiful sister resting in my arms and I was loving it.

I dosed off, while lying on the couch. When I woke up at about 10:00 PM, there was nothing, but snow on the TV screen. Then I noticed that Renee fell asleep also. I started rubbing the top of her head gently, while whispering,

Baby wake up.

Minutes later, Renee woke up whining like a baby.

"Ok, I'm up boo."

She got up from the couch and looked at the clock on the wall, and said.

"Damn it's late, excuse me for a minute, while I put on my pajamas."

She went into her bedroom for a brief minute, and then into the bathroom. While she was in the shower, I got up from the couch, to turn off the VCR. I flipped through a few channels, but nothing was on TV. I heard the water turning off in the bathroom, so I quickly turned off the TV and sat back down on the couch. Renee came out of the bathroom, and into the living room.

"Why is it so dark in here?" she asked.

There was nothing on TV, so I turned it off.

She went back into her bedroom to finish getting dressed. Five minutes later, I heard the intro of "I Knew it had to be you" by TROOP. Then Renee came back into the living room, wearing a one-piece pajama outfit. She looked just like a child. The only thing that was missing, were the connecting feet, with the white vinyl bottoms. I was sitting up in the middle of the couch.

Renee walked over to me and sat on my lap, she straddled her legs over mine. Then she lifted up my head, and we made eye contact. She started kissing me in a way that I have never experienced before. Renee grabbed my right hand,

and placed it through the buttons on her pajamas. I started caressing her body gently with one hand, while slowly moving down to her navel, with my other hand. I moved my hand a little lower and said to myself

Damn, she aint got on no panties.

As soon as I said that, I felt myself rising. Renee grabbed my shirt; from around the bottom of my waste and whispered in my ear

"Lift up."

I raised my butt from off of the shirt, and held my hands in the air. Renee lifted my shirt over my head slowly, and then she kissed me all over my chest.

I was ready to explode.

She took my pager off my pants and placed it on the coffee table. Then She undid my belt, followed by the buttons on my jeans. I lifted up, while she slid my pants down. Then I unfastened the buttons on her pajamas and began to kiss her breast. She had the prettiest nipples I had ever seen. At that point I was ready.

Renee, take this off I said.

I was, referring to her pajamas that were in my way. She leaned up off of me, to remove her pajamas. I followed her, still kissing her breast, but now I had worked my way down to her navel. She placed her hand gently on my shoulders, and said

"Come here."

As I stood up, she began to lie down on the sofa. Renee had her left leg raised up on the back of the sofa with her foot touching the wall. I paused for a minute, and looked her body up and down slowly.

Damn all this for me?

"Only if you want it," she answered.

I gently laid down, in between Renee's legs. At the beginning I was a little nervous, and I must have been moving too fast, cause Renee said

"Boo slow down, take your time, it aint going nowhere."

Then I started to get this tingling feeling traveling all the way from my legs and up through my back, and my booty cheeks got tighter. I started screaming her name.

"REENNEEE"

She held me tighter. Once I was finish I lifted myself off of her, and looked for my boxers. Renee got up and went into the bathroom, later returning with two washcloths. After I was done cleaning myself, I looked at my pager for the time.

Damn it's 1:00?

"Yes Boo."

Baby I don't want to leave, but I gotta take my mother her car.

We got dressed, and then we sat back down on the couch and held each other for a minute. After a few minutes had past Renee said

"You better take your mother her car."

Yeah, you're right I responded softly.

We got up from off the couch, and Renee walked me to the door and kissed me goodnight. I drove home straight down Bailey Ave. I couldn't stop smiling the whole way home. That night, I was like a kid in the candy store. I rushed into the house, and straight to the shower. As soon as I got out of the shower, I called Renee to let her know that I had made it home safely. We both laughed and joked on the phone for a while. Then we said our I love you's and goodnight's and hung up the phone.

The loving was definitely too much for me to handle, and as a result, Renee was pregnant a couple of months after we began having sex. I was nineteen at the time, and she was seventeen. Both of our parents stood behind us, in our decision to keep our child. Besides, having an abortion was not an option that we were familiar with nor did we consider it.

I was a very happy father to be. Renee was very happy also, and she looked so good pregnant. We started purchasing things for our baby, and our parents did too. In August of 1994 I moved in with Renee and her mother. We would stay up late at night, trying to decide on what we would name our child. We decide on "Malik" if it's a boy, and "Michay" if it's a girl.

During her pregnancy Renee and I would argue constantly. Everyday I would find out something else regarding Renee's past. What made it hurt worst is that, I had to hear about these thing's from everyone except my Renee. I would curse her out, call her a liar, and then break up with her. This type of behavior continued throughout her entire pregnancy.

A little while after Renee and I started dating, I had quit my job at the restaurant. I got another job at Kaufman's Department Store. While I was working there, I met a white woman named Jackie. Jackie was 28 and she only dated black men, and the darker the better, so I was definitely a suspect. Jackie never had any problems attracting the brother's either. She was real cute and she was built like a sister. She basically lived in the gym, snow white kept that body in shape. When we first started to talk to each other, Jackie used to tell me stories about her boyfriend that she just broke up with.

She said that he used to whip her ass daily, and one time he even sent her to work with a black eye. Jackie and I used to talk for a while. I was honest and straight up with her from day one. I told her about Renee, and there was no replacing her. She understood, and we both agreed to do like R-Kelly, and "keep it on the down low." Jackie would come by my mother's house and pick me up, and we would go to the movie's way out. I remember one day I took her so far, that we got lost on our way back. I couldn't risk someone from the hood seeing us together. My mother told me to stop seeing her, she didn't like the idea of me being with an older woman, she said, but I think it was the fact that she was white that really bothered her. I mean I was only 17 at the time, but I knew how to treat a lady, and that's what Jackie liked about me. Not long after we met, Jackie told me that she likes her man to wear boxers, and she handed me a bag with like ten pairs inside.

I remember one night after Jackie had moved into a new apartment on the east side, she invited me over late one night. When I got there, we sat and talked for a while, and then she ran me a bubble bath, and washed me up. At age 17, I was definitely doing the most. You couldn't tell me shit. After I got out the tub, she slipped on something real sexy, and we fell asleep in the room on the bed. When I woke up I was naked on the couch and Jackie and her roommate both was walking around naked also. I sat up for a minute, trying to remember what the hell went on that night, but I couldn't come up with anything. Then Renee walked her naked ass in the living room while I was sitting on the couch with Jackie. She rubbed my head and asked me was I staying for breakfast. I began to get mad because there is no way that a woman is going to be cool with her roommate walking around naked while her man was in the house. Jackie didn't say anything, and they were both giggling like they had just finished running a train on me. I was still young at the time and if it was to go down like that, I wanted to be awake, or at least be able to remember what happened. I was pissed, and their laughter was pissing me off. I demanded that Jackie take me home, and after that day, we didn't speak to each other for a week.

We met again after that little episode was behind us and we were sitting in front of my mother's house talking. We talked the night away, and before I knew anything, it was 7:00 AM and my mother was pulling down the street. My mother pulled in the driveway and me and Jackie waved at her. I knew that she was pissed, because she didn't even wave back. She just gave me a mean ass stare. I was trying to wrap the conversation up, then, all of a sudden my mother came running out the driveway.

"Get out the car bitch."

Mom what's going on? Why you buggin?

"You get in the house before I kick your ass too."

Goodnight Jackie, I'll talk to you later.

As I was leaving my mother jumped on the hood of Jackie's car.

"What's up bitch, why you over here bothering my son?"

"Don't come around here no more."

My mother got off her car and Jackie pulled off flying down the street.

CHAPTER 4
MY FIRST ARREST

The first time that I got "knocked" was in August of 1994. I was nineteen years old at the time, and still living in Buffalo, NY. I had been lying on the floor in my mother's house, with my shirt off, trying to catch a breeze, when my pager went off and woke me up, at about 6:30 PM. It was this "Hype" named Freddy. When I called back, he was like

"Are you holding?"

I said, no doubt, what you need?

"Come through, I got fifty to spend."

Give me about an hour, I said, and then we hung up.

I immediately jumped up and called my mother to see if she was on her way home with the car. She answered her phone at work, and soon as I mentioned use of the car, she started going off on me.

"Don't be making plans in my car, you don't know what I have to do when I get off work."

All you have to do is say yes or no mama.

"I'm coming straight home, to get dressed for the concert and I don't have time to be calling all around town trying to find you, and my car.

"What concert? I asked.

She said that she was going to see Luther, and I could use the car while she gets dressed.

After I hung up the phone with my mother, Renee called. She was asking me to bring her something to eat. I asked her, what did she want? She said a hoagie. I told her to call and order it, and I would pick it up, when I went out. I hung up the phone, and went to my stash to get my "bundle." Freddy was alright with me, so I figured I would show him some love, by picking out a nice size rock for him. I found a piece, took it out of the bundle and wrapped it up in foil. Then I looked at the clock on the wall and it read 8:00 PM. My mother should've been home. I knew that Freddy liked my "product," but I also knew he wasn't going to wait on it forever. I was anxiously pacing back and forth, from the kitchen to the living room. About ten minutes later, my mother pulled into the driveway. I grabbed my coat and rushed out the door.

Wait! I'm leaving out mom.

As she put the car in park and started to gather her things, she said,

"You need to start looking for yourself a car."

Ok mom.

Then I closed the door and drove off. When I got to the corner, I reached in my pocket and pulled out my DJ Clue mix tape. I popped it in and started adjusting the bass. I got the sounds right and went on my way. I made a left down Hewitt Ave, and then a right on Bailey. I slowed up at the sound of my name being called by my man Greg in front of the corner store. I pulled the car over, and parked. Greg jumped in and left the door open. He then asked me where I was going, I told him I was going to take care of some business and I would be right back.

"Pull off, here comes "one time.""

He closed his door and then I started to pull off.

"Irk" "Irk,"

The "Narco's" were in an unmarked Buick with their lights flashing on us. I'm sitting in the car like

Damn, this can't be happening.

They came up to the car looked in, and called Greg by his first name and told him to step out the car. The other officer, then asked me where I was going? I told him to pick up a pizza for my mother.

Then he said, "Are you holding?"

I don't know what you mean by holding sir.

"Step out the car."

I got out and he started to search me. He was almost done, and then he reached into the pocket on my right, and pulled out the bundle of foil.

"What's this?"

At that time I said officer take me down, but please don't impound my mother's car.

It took a lot of begging, but I finally convinced him. At that point, I wasn't worried about going to jail. I was more concerned about my mother missing a Luther concert. That was grounds for her to commit murder. She would kill me, two times. She had another set of keys, so I figured that she could get a ride around the corner to pick up the car. The officer cuffed me while his other partner locked my mother's car and turned off the lights.

As I was sitting in the back seat of the police car, my man Jay rode by looking in on me. I told him to go by the house and tell my mother to come and get the car. He pulled off and I suspect that he went straight to my mother's house to tell her. As soon as we arrived at central booking, while we were walking down the hall, an officer asked

"Are you guys bringing in a Michael Martin?"

My arresting officer said "yeah, why?"

"His mother's on the phone."

I just shook my head and said damn.

My uncle was a cop and I was just hoping that he was off that evening. Luckily he was, but he still called the officers who arrested me that night. Right after I checked in my property, the officer started to give me the change your life around speech. He said

" You have a lot of people, who care about you, so we're going to give you a break."

I just sat there listening to him, and then he escorted me to the elevator, up to the tenth floor, and into my cell.

I just sat there thinking damn; I'm in the system.

It was now about 1:00 AM, and the deputy just finished finger printing me. About twenty minutes later, he came back to my cell and yelled out for it to be opened.

What's going on? I asked.

"You're free to go, and here is your appearance ticket."

When he walked me down to the front door, my mother was standing there all dressed up.

She looked good, but I could tell that she was "heated."

We walked out the door and I couldn't even look her in the eye. She went on about

"Drugs can only do two things for you."

"Kill you

Or

Get you killed."

I just let her have her say that night,

Besides, I was a little upset at the fact that she went not only to the concert, but also to the after party. She did all this and then came down to get me out of jail. My mother got me a good lawyer named Sal. He was Italian and madd cool. When we first met

He said

"I'm going to get this case dismissed, but in the meantime I need you to stay off the block for a while."

"Lay low, till this thing is over."

I agreed, and after two court appearances, Sal held up his part of the bargain, and got the charges dismissed.

CHAPTER 5
WHAT'S A BROTHA TO DO?

Why is it that when you have girlfriend, every woman wants you? I couldn't beg for a date, prior to meeting Renee, now, women are coming out of the woodwork for me. I ran into my old girlfriend Liz at the grocery store one day. I had to leave Liz alone when we were in high school because she was trying to put a brotha on "lockdown," I definitely couldn't have that. Liz's appearance hadn't changed at all. She was still thick, and sexy as hell. Liz also had long pretty hair that just enhanced her beautiful smile.

When I seen her in the store, she was holding a baby, that she later introduced as her six month old son. Her baby's father was some kid that she met while in high school, after I wouldn't settle down with her. He wouldn't present a problem for me though because he was currently in jail, for some drug charges. We talked for a while and then we exchanged phone numbers. I had to give her the digits to my mother's house and my pager number because I was still shacking up with Renee. Liz calling Renee's house would land me in the hospital.

We finally talked to each other on the phone, and before I knew it, we were spending an awful amount of time together. Her son was real cool, and I loved spending time with the both of them. Liz was having some family problems, so she had temporarily moved in with her mentor Jackie. Jackie had a daughter named Shante, who knew my girlfriend Renee. Renee and Shante had fought a few years ago over some guy, who had them both sprung. At the mention of the others name all you would hear is

"I hate that bitch."

Buffalo was a small town, so Renee would always get word that my car was parked in front of Shante's house for hours. My pager would go off and, every time that I would call Renee back she would say,

"How could you do this to me? You know I hate that girl."

I told Renee that I wasn't there with Shante.

At the same time I failed to mention anything about Liz. I guess that was a little pay back from all of her rumors hurting me. I began to play mind games with her, like she used to do with me.

Renee would curse me out daily, and tell me that she hated me. Liz and I would talk for hours at a time, and she was always there when I needed someone to listen to me. That was something that I was no longer getting at home, and I had to get it from somewhere. Liz had a son, and had been hurt by most of the men in her life. I too had issues that I was dealing with myself. I still had a lot of feelings for Renee, and I was still living with her. I was basically calling out to Renee, by being with Liz, or so I thought.

As I continued spending more time with Liz, I became good friends with Shante and her mother Jackie. Shante and I started to go out a lot but, we were just friends. Later Shante told me that she wanted to talk to my boy Emery. Emery was the pretty boy out of my crew. He had many sista's, weak at the knees. Emery started hanging out with Shante. Not long after that, Shante introduced me to one of her girlfriends named Rejoice.

The name definitely fit the sista. At the sight of this woman that is just what she made a brotha do, "Rejoyce." She also introduced me to this other sista named Andrea. Between the two of them, how could a brotha be so lucky?

Andrea was tall, beautiful and intelligent. She had a caramel complexion, and she was a dancer. Rejoyce on the other hand, was medium height with long pretty hair and green eyes that was given to her at birth.

Whenever Emery and Shante wanted to hook up, Shante would call both Rejoyce, and Andrea, to see who was game. I spent more time with Rejoyce because Andrea was really into her studies, so she wouldn't be willing to hang out as much, only on weekends. Rejoyce was just the opposite. She attended an all girls private school; so when it was time to unwind and get loose, she did just that. Liz and Renee were still in the picture, while all of this was going on, but they knew nothing. If I wasn't out with Shante and one of her friends, then I was laying up with Renee or Liz. Let's just say I played my cards right—or so I thought.

CHAPTER 6
VALENTINES DAY 1995

That Valentine's Day I was wore out. Being a player is hard work. I had to get teddy bears, cards, and candy for five women. Renee and I woke up expressing our feelings for each other. The baby was due any day now, but it is too true about what they say regarding [pregnant coochie], so I had to go there. I got dressed and went on with my day. I kept all of the valentine gifts in the trunk of my car because Renee was "nosey."

I met Rejoyce at her house after she came home from school. To my surprise, she had a little something for me too. I didn't stay long because I had a lot of deliveries to make, so we ended it on a hug, and I told her we would talk later. Afterwards, I went over to Shante's house to chill with Liz. Once I was there, I gave Shante her gift, and one for her to give to Andrea. Of course I had to do it on the sneak, otherwise I would have to hear Liz's mouth. I wasn't trying to do that, so I played it off by telling Shante to get the bags that she left in my car, out of the trunk.

Renee started paging me about thirty minutes later, so I had to go home for a minute. I got my hug from Liz, and then one from Shante. Liz wasn't too happy about that last hug, but who cares? I went home and took a little nap. I woke up, at the sound of my pager going off.

"Call the bitch back," yelled Renee.

What are you talking about?

"You know what the hell I'm talking about, them hoes only call because they know you're with me."

First I don't know any hoes, and if you are referring to my friends, then you have nothing to worry about because they know you are my girl.

"Well give me your pager and let me call the bitch back,"

I'm not about to play these games with you Renee.

I got up, threw on my sweats, and timbs, grabbed my keys and bounced.

She continued to shout, but I wasn't hearing her.

I figured; she would get over it.

I hopped in the car and pulled over at the corner to use the payphone. I called the number back, and it was my man

Emery. He was over one of his new girl's house. He quickly asked me

"What's up with Shante?"

Shit, she's at the crib, meet me over there.

"Cool, I'm on my way."

We hung up the phone, and I started driving to Shante's house.

We both pulled up at Shante's house, right around the same time. As soon as we walked in, Shante jumped on Emery and gave him a big hug and a kiss. Then she went back into her room and came back out the door with MADD flower's, some chocolate, and a card for Emery.

We both looked at each other like damn. I didn't have to worry about Liz acting up that night because she stayed the night at one of her girlfriend's house. Shante had cooked, so we ate dinner, watched TV, laughed and joked all night. It was getting late, and I knew that Shante wanted to be alone with Emery.

I told them that I was about to bounce, and that I would be back later.

Then Emery jumped up and said don't leave yet; I need to talk to you.

Emery was a little slow, and I guess he wasn't getting the picture that night.

Before I knew it, we all fell asleep on Shante's bed while looking at photo's.

Jackie woke up and came in the room at about 6:00 am.

Prior to this, I thought she too was gone for the night. She called Shante out of the room to speak to her. I could tell by her tone, that she was not pleased with her daughter entertaining two men. It didn't matter that nothing happened with any of us, it was just the principal behind the whole idea, and I agreed with her mother's reaction. We got up and went back to my mother's house, to finish getting some sleep. My mother was working mornings, so it was cool, and besides, I wouldn't have to hear her mouth about me running the streets, and how I needed to be in somebody's church.

The next day, Renee cursed me out. I forgot that I told her that I would be right back. Then she went on, asking me

What the hell was I doing spending the night over Shante's house.

Damn this town is too small, she finds out my every move.

Then she started cursing and crying. She was telling me how I was stressing her out, and that she was pregnant. We cut the conversation short, and I asked Emery what he was about to do, and then I went over Renee's house.

Chapter 7
My First Daughter Is Born

On February 24, 1995 Renee gave birth to a six pound, eight ounce baby girl. We named her Michay. She was beautiful and we were both very happy. I told her that I was finish playing games, and that we would be a family.

Hey, it sounded good.

I took pictures of the whole childbirth. I was really caught up in the moment. I guess that's why I made that comment to Renee about us being a family. Right after Michay was born, the three of us moved into my mother's house. Renee and her mother had not been getting along, and that was nothing new. Everyday, they would be arguing about something. I always remained neutral, when they had their differences. Renee was still a child whether she wanted to admit it or not. She was never willing to accept criticism from anyone, including her mother.

She felt that she had her own child and her own money, so no one could tell her "Shit." Since that was the case, her mother felt like; if you know it all, then maybe you need to be out on your own.

Now I was in a very stressful situation, living with my mother. At that time my mother and I didn't see eye to eye, on issues in my life. She was constantly preaching work or school.

I had to get money, by any means necessary. After about a week the fact that I was living back with my mom really bothered me. I wasn't feeling the situation at all, so I started looking high and low, for a new job.

CHAPTER 8
"CABBIE"

There was an ad in the newspaper for cab drivers. That said, "for consideration, apply in person at Cold Springs Taxi Service at 234 Northampton St." The Cold Spring area was not your typical residential community. The average annual income for families living in the area was about $30,000 a year. Drugs, and the crime that they brought with them, really took a toll on the neighborhood. I went to speak to Mr. Thomas, who at the time owned Cold Spring Taxi Service. I told him that I was very interested in becoming a cab driver.

I immediately sensed hesitation on his part, as soon as I told him that I was 19 yrs old.

He said that I would be a big insurance risk for him, but he would give me a shot anyway. I immediately began the licensing process, and the actual driver training. I trained with a gentleman named Murphy. He was an old player who didn't talk to women over 25. He was a real player, and the one to put me up on game regarding cabs, women, hustling and pimping. Murphy was my mentor and I think about the fun we had all the time. My training lasted about one week, the same amount of time that it took for me to get my license. After training for an additional week, I was able to lease my own cab. My cab number was fifteen. As soon as it was issued to me, I had some business cards made, with my cab number and two phone numbers where I could be reached for service. My mother hated the fact that I was a cab driver.

She would say that it was too dangerous.

I would always respond to her by saying that,

I'm a young black male; life in itself is dangerous for me.

My mother and no one else could change my mind about my new job. I loved being a cab driver. It was fun, entertaining, and I met a lot of very interesting people. Initially Renee was cool with my new job, but then as usual, she started bugging. She accused me of never calling my pages back, and being too busy for her and my daughter. I never said anything to defend myself, because I felt it was useless. I would just ignore her, occasionally say whatever, or just leave out when she started to complain.

One night while I was dropping off a fare, I received a call on the radio. The dispatcher said that it was a young lady, and she only wanted to be picked up by me. I asked for the address and proceeded to the house. As soon as I pulled up and hit the horn, three sisters came out the door. I couldn't see them that well because it was really dark.

As they got closer to the car, I realized that it was Shante, Andrea, and Rejoyce. We all had lost contact with one another. After Emery continued to show no interest, Shante decided to move on. Rejoyce started seeing this kid named George from my old neighborhood, and Andrea was getting ready to move to Atlanta. Shante and I would talk every once in a while, but it was nothing like it used to be. I was actually happy to see them. I hopped out of the car and started to give them all a hug. I hugged Andrea last.

Andrea always held a brotha in a way that would keep him thinking about her for days. We got into the car, and we kicked it, like we hadn't seen each other in years. I took Andrea home last that night, because I wanted another one of those hugs. I got one and even a little kiss on the cheek, so I was set for the night.

After I got back into the car, I took a drive over my man Teeter's house. Teeter about the same age as me, but he had paper, that I could only dream about. Teeter had been hustling since he was like thirteen. Every once in a while, he would be with my brother Mark. Whenever you seen them two together, you just knew that it was about paper because Mark usually rolled solo, or with one of his many women. People, who didn't know Teeter like that, used to always say that he was "shady" and not to be trusted. It was usually the ones who were shook by him or his crew. Teeter and his lil shorties were no joke; they would put two in your dome with the quickness. Teeter was all about money and taking care of his family.

I can recall this time when Teeter rented my cab for one hour, to take his whole crew to the mall. He let them go through the mall and get whatever they wanted.

I had seen something in Teeter that most cats never paid attention to. I felt that Teeter was really paying for acceptance, and in a very big way. He was looking for love in all the wrong places.

In the streets, there is no love, and that's what he failed to realize.

His family loved him and so did I, with or without the money. Teeter pumped weed out of this house on Goodloe St. It was almost closing time, so I gave him a ride to stash his paper. Afterwards, we kicked it for about an hour. We sat and questioned each other, about our lives, and was this what life was all about? After a while, I began to get tired, so I dropped Teeter off at his grandmother's house, and then I went home.

CHAPTER 9
DON'T BOTHER MY FAMILY

One night in March of 1996 I came back home from a long day in my cab at about 8:00 PM. We were living in the apartment above Renee's grandmother and her fathers' home at the time. I figured I could get some sleep and go back out later. When I got home, Renee was sitting in the chair feeding my daughter. They looked so beautiful together. I gave the both of them a kiss.

Baby, wake me up in two hours, so I can go back to work.

"Why you can't never stay home with your family?"

Because I have bills to pay.

"Well I'm tired of this, you need to stay home sometimes."

Ok, I will stay home tomorrow night; now wake me up in two hours.

"Whatever."

She woke me up at about 10:00 PM. I took a bath and changed my clothes before I went out that night. By the time I was done, Michay was already asleep, so Renee walked me to the door. As soon as we went down the stairs, Renee jumped on me and I carried her down the stairs. We got to the end of the stairs, then in the driveway to my taxi. Renee got in the passenger side to kiss me. After she was done giving me a kiss, she walked back towards the door. Her father showed up, drunk as usual. Renee felt that he was never a father to her, so she showed very little respect towards him. And she had a very smart ass mouth, so that made matters worse. We both played him real short whenever he spoke, because it was usually the liquor and not him speaking.

"What the hell yaw out here doing this time of night?"

"What? Look dad, you're drunk and I'm really not in the mood."

"Who in the hell do you think you're talking to?"

"I'm talking to you and you better get out my face."

Hey, what's going on? Yaw both cool out. Renee, go upstairs.

"Look, you mind your business, this is my daughter, and I say what goes around here."

Whatever, Baby just go upstairs.

"I can't he has my arm."

"Bring your ass here, you're going to start respecting me."

"Fuck you, you aint my father, and get off my arm."

I had left for a minute, thinking that Renee was headed up the stairs, but the arguing seemed to be escalating, so I went to the back hallway stairs to see what was going on.

"Hey I thought I told yaw to cool out."

As I spoke, I looked up and Renee was off her feet, being choked by her father. You could barely hear the words "get off me" coming out of her mouth. I rushed to my taxi, reached in my glove box and grabbed my deuce-five. I jumped back out of the car, leaving the door open and then to the back door. When I returned he was banging her back and forth against the second floor window.

Get your damn hands off my woman.

He didn't respond, so I fired a shot, then another and one after that. I seen him bend over reaching, so I thought he was going for his gun. He was never without his four-fifth, so I kept shooting, chasing him through the house. When I got to the front of the house, I had emptied the clip, and the chamber had slid back and my toast was smoking. I ran back out the back door, passing Renee.

"I love you, where are you going to go."

I'm going to work. I will call you later.

I jumped in my taxi, threw the gun on the seat and with all the excitement I pulled off, leaving the door open.

"BAM"

The door hit the side of the house and was dented in so bad that it couldn't close.

Damn, I can't go to work like this.

I pulled the car out to the street, put it in drive and sped away. I was hitting corners like my last name was Andretti. I drove to the cabstand, where I dropped my taxicab off, and jumped in my friends taxi and got a ride to my grandparent's house.

I stashed the gun right before I went to my grandparents house. When I entered the house, I went downstairs, my aunt Ray lived there. She must've seen the look in my eye,

"Baby what's wrong?"

Auntie I think I just killed somebody

"Where? Who?"

Renee's father at the house, he was beating on her, and I warned him to stop, but he wouldn't, so I shot him and I kept trying to shoot him.

"Well, we better call your lawyer. What's Sal's number."

By this time my grandfather had heard all the noise, so he came rushing down the stairs. I couldn't even look him in the eye.

"What's going on?"

My auntie spoke up, while she was waiting for someone to answer the phone at my lawyer's house.

"Dad, he done shot the girls father, and he thinks he's dead."

"Boy, now what the hell you go and do a thing like that for?"

"He says the man was beating on her, he was just protecting his family."

"Shush, I can't hear."

"Hello, I'm sorry to wake you, but this is Michael's aunt Ray, we have a problem."

She told my lawyer the whole story, and he told me to turn myself in, and he would be down to the jail in the morning.

My grandfather went upstairs and threw on his clothes, to take me to central booking.

"Well come on, let's go."

We walked out the door and got in the car. As soon as we pulled out the driveway, and went to the corner, the police was coming in the opposite direction.

"They're on the way to the house to get you, duck down."

I laid down in the back seat, so that I couldn't be noticed in the car.

We entered the expressway, and went straight to Central Booking.

Chapter 10
Back In The System

As soon as we arrived, an officer who was also a friend of the family, came outside searched me, and ensured my grandfather that everything would be ok.

I was processed and fingerprinted and then placed in my cell. The whole time that I was in there, all that I thought about was Renee and my daughter. I also thought about what took place that night, and how my life was going to change now.

The guards came and got me out of my cell for court at about 6:30 AM. We all went over to court, and when the deputy came to get me, I just knew that it was over. The judge looked over a few of her papers, and said

"How does the defendant plead?"

She was starring me in the eye while addressing my lawyer.

"Not guilty, your honor."

"Well in light of the seriousness of this crime I am going to set bail at $100,000.

I just looked back at Renee, and over to my mother, for I knew that I would not see them for a while.

I went back to the holding cell, then to the county jail. I sat in a smoke filled room, that shouldn't have been considering that there was a law passed, banning cigarette smoke in correctional institutions. I sat there in prison watching inmates pilled on top of each other as we all sat in a room the size of a kitchen pantry. Along with the cigarette smoke, one of the inmates was able to retrieve a couple of pieces of crack, from a place that I would rather not mention right now. So, I'm sitting in this cell thinking of my family; while people argue over who's hogging the stem, and the lookout is threatened to watch out for the guards.

So this is what jail is all about?

Finally after having to wait for 12 hours, a deputy came to get me. I went to take a shower and get my bedding and linen. I was then sent to the gym. The jail was overcrowded, so they were housing prisoners in the gym. I went in and found a spot in the corner, where I laid my mat down and got settled for the night. The TV went off about two hours later, and then it was lights out.

I really didn't get any sleep that night, but who could blame me? It wasn't like I was staying the night in Trump Towers. The next morning at 5:00 AM the Guards brought breakfast. That was around the time that sleep kicked in for my body, so I would just drink my hot coffee, and go back to sleep.

When I finally woke up at about 11:00 AM, I went into the bathroom to wash up. The guys were telling me that the "deps" only took them to the showers once a week. After hearing that, I figured out why the gym smelled like collard greens. I had to wash out my underclothes by hand. There was a dirty clothes hamper for me to put them in. Once I returned to my bunk, there were new prisoners coming in.

One of the guys yelled out my name, and said What's up. Once I was able to get a good look at him, it was this kid I knew from around the way. He came over to my mat, and we just kicked it for a minute. He had heard all about what happened to me, and why I was arrested. He then told me that he got arrested for strong arm robbery, but he proclaimed his innocence, he said he was just to drunk to argue. He later added that he took a swing at the arresting officers; and that's what really landed him here. Lunch was around 12:30 PM. I only ate one of the sandwiches and packed the rest up in my pillowcase with my leftovers from breakfast. I ate very little, so that I could trade some of my goods later on, if I needed to. I didn't know how long I was going to be in, so I had to prepare for the bit.

Right before dinner, the "Dep" came and got me, because I had a visitor. Before I was allowed to sit at the table, I had to go into a little room and be strip searched, and told the rules of the visiting room. There was to be no touching at all. Only a brief hug was acceptable. No holding hands, and no tongue action during a kiss. Failure to follow these rules meant severe punishment and you would receive no more visits.

As soon as I made it into the room, I saw Renee, and my auntie Rita from California. I just smiled with joy outside, but in the inside, I was really sad. I never wanted to receive any more visits after that, and that's just what I told them. All men have a soft side, and in a jail, that can easily be taken advantage of. The visit made me weak, and I couldn't risk letting that happen again. I had sat down and my auntie started with the questions.

"How are they treating you?"

I'm ok, I have a few people's from the outside in here with me, and I'm eating good.

"I brought Michay, she's outside with your grandfather."

Don't ever bring my daughter down here again, this is no place for a child.

"Ok, but I thought you might want to see her."

Not here, when I get out.

"Well yaw calm down, and lets spend this time together while we have it."

That goes for the visits too, tell everyone that I'm not taking anymore visits.

"Ok, but why?"

It makes me sad, and I don't want anyone to see me like this.

"Well let's say a prayer, and then we are going to leave ok?"

We all bowed our heads as my auntie began to pray. I don't exactly remember the words, but I do know that it was a soothing prayer, and one that I really needed.

After I was done with my visit, I went in the room to be strip searched again, and then back to the gym. Shortly after I arrived, we were served dinner. I ate all of it and I drank my chocolate milk that I had saved from breakfast. Seven days later I went back to appear before the judge. The night before I prayed all night that the judge would be sick. When I went down to get dressed for court, a deputy called out my name and gave me a suit and my shoes. My mother and lawyer felt that I had to change my appearance to collaborate with their portrayal of me as no danger or threat to society. I went in the room and changed, and when I stepped out, I definetley got the approval from the inmates, cause they were all starring. We loaded the bus, and were on our way to the court building. Once we made it to the court house, we were placed in cells until our case was called. From the time that I woke up I just kept telling myself that the judge wasn't going to be in today. A couple of people went before me, but one came back. As soon as he came back he said.

"She's not in, they said she was sick, there's some cool judge out there, since the jails were overcrowded, he was letting everybody go."

I just smiled, because my prayers were answered.

The deputy finally came and called my name. When I came out of the cell the dep looked me up and down.

"Brotha I've been working here for 12 years, and I have never seen anyone as clean as you."

Thank you sir.

"You did the smart thing. Some of these fools come in here and go in front of the judge with there pants hanging off their ass, and then they wonder why they didin't get released."

Yes sir.

We had reached the court and he took me inside and sat me down.

"Good luck little bro."

Thanks.

I sat down and looked around, the court room was full of my supporters. My grandmother and grandfather was there, Renee's mother, Renee, my auntie, and my grandfather on my mother's side of the family, and my mother; sat there watching to see if I would be released, or the bail would be reduced.

My lawyer walked up to the podium with me and continued to plead.

"Your honor, Mr. Martin has the support of his family and his mother who works for the state is present in the courtroom today. Mr. Martin has a job driving taxi and he's a family man. We ask that he be released on his own recognizant."

The Prosecuting attorney argued that I was a menace to society, and that I commited a very serious crime. The last word's came from the judge, so I didn't pay the prosecuter any attention.

The room was silenced and then the judge spoke.

"Mr. Martin you are dressed pretty sharp today, and you don't strike me as a violent individual. I think you made a mistake and I'm going to release you, but I want you to stay away from the victim. And you must make all of your scheduled court appearances, or I will issue a warrant for your arrest. Are we clear?"

Yes Sir.

I was a free man. I was so happy. I went out of the courtroom and said hello to everyone, thanked them for their support, and gave them a hug. I couldn't look my grandfather in the eye though. He looked at me and said,

"Bo, pick your head up off the ground, there ain't nothing to be shame for. Everybody makes mistakes, but it's what we do after we have made them that's important. Now hold your head high, and be a man."

Once I was done speaking to my grandfather, my mother took me to the jail to retrieve my property. After I had my property, my mother took me over to my house. I walked in, barely speaking to Renee, and just grabbed a few of my things.

"Where are you going?"

I'm going to stay with my mother for a while, it's best for everybody.

"What about me and Michay? We need you here."

Renee, I will call you and we will talk about it later.

I left the house and went home with my mother. As soon as I went into the house, my sister gave me a big hug.

There is definitely no place like home.

CHAPTER 11

MARIE

Since the shooting my relationship with Renee had really gone downhill. She was upset because I was never available to spend time with her. I had partially blamed Renee for making me feel the way that I did about her, and causing me to act out in such a way that would definitely change my life forever. I had started back driving taxi in my spare time and staying with Renee over her mother's house every once in a while. My aunt owned a home on Best street, but she had moved out six months ago. I lived there, so that no one would break in or vandalize the house.

On my twenty-first birthday, I was pulling up in the front of my house. The minute that I stopped the car; my neighbor's son was all over it with ice cream all over his hands. He was like three years old at the time, and very curious. He immediately got my attention and started asking me questions.

"What does this button do?" He asked.

That's for the treble, and the one next to it is for bass, I responded.

Once I started to get out of the car, his mother called him.

"Jason, leave that man's car alone"

Then she spoke to me, and asked how I was doing.

I responded fine, then I smiled and walked into my house.

I went out later that evening, and she was sitting on the stoop, in the same position as earlier.

"Hello, my name is Marie"

Hello, my name is Michael.

"I know."

What's that suppose to mean?

"It's nothing to worry about let's just say that, I did my homework."

Our conversation, went back and forth like this for hours. I had really lost track of time. I looked at my watch, and she must have picked up on my gesture.

"Do you have to go?"

Yeah, I got to go and take care of something real quick.

"Well it was nice talking to you, and you don't have to be a stranger."

Ok, I will keep that in mind.

I left for a couple of hours. As soon I was pulling up she was coming over towards the driveway to get in her car.

Are you leaving me?

"No I'm just going around the corner, to put a number in."

"Why? Are you going to take me?"

Sure, I will give you a ride; hop in.

She got in the car, and I helped her adjust the seat.

"Don't be playing that music all loud in my ear please."

What are you talking about I don't play my music loud.

"Yes you do."

"I know when you pull up, cause my son goes to the window, when he hears the bass." Really, he does all that?

What do you do?

Do you follow him to the window also?

I was flirting strong, and she knew it.

We both just looked at each other and laughed. We had arrived at the store, so she got out of the car. About ten minutes later she returned, and said,

"You know, you have a nice car."

I'm glad you like it. I aims to please.

We both just laughed.

I was bumping Rock Wit Me, by Freddie Jackson on the stereo that night.

"What you know about this?" she said, referring to the song.

More than you could imagine.

"You don't know the type of imagination, that I have then"

I just looked at her and she looked back at me with this devilish grin.

We had arrived back at her house by now.

"What are you about to do?"

I was going to come on your porch and finish our conversation.

"Ok, well come on, and keep me company."

Baby didn't waste no time. As soon as we sat down, Marie was like,

"Tell me a little something about yourself."

Like what?

"Whatever's on your mind."

How about what's on yours?

"You already, know what's on mine."

What's that?

"You."

Before I could inquire a little further, she said,

"I have been watching you for a while; but you weren't ready yet."

And now I am?

"Yes, but it's really up to you."

I began to look her up and down again.

Marie was madd thick, and I was told that she too pays, like she weights. Marie was also much older, a veteran in the game. She kept herself together, and her kids looking good too. She wasn't one of the mother's that I was starting to see a lot of lately.

The ones, who are geared down, but their kids look like, who did it and why.

We continued to talk and I told her my age, which she said, she already knew. Then she told me that she was thirty-three, and she was almost married once. She told me the story about how her husband to be, had a little too much fun at his bachelor party. I told her about Renee, and a few other women that I was seeing at the time.

I wanted her to know from the start, what she was getting herself into.

Besides, she lived next door, and claimed to have done her homework. So I figured that she already knew how I got down.

We went at it for hours, talking about everything. It was about 1:00 AM when I left.

I went back over Renee's house and she was doing the usual. As soon as I stepped in the house she started asking me,

Where have I been? And why I didn't call her back, when she was paging me.

I had noticed her first page, and then just ignored the rest.

The conversation with Marie was going too well.

CHAPTER 12
ATTRACTED TO AN OLDER WOMAN

Marie and I continued to see each other on a regular. This was the first time that I have ever dated an older woman. Jackie didn't count. We had the coolest relationship. My whole crew envied me. Marie would fix me breakfast, lunch, and dinner. While all of this was going on, I was still working things out with Renee, but I wasn't about to miss this opportunity to be with Marie.

When we would go out to a mall or to any store for that matter. Marie would never let me spend my money. I was treated like a king. She spoiled me rotten. We were not living together, at least not at this point, but I still lived next door. Whenever I wanted to spend the night, all I had to do is go over her house. I had my own key to Marie's house. She gave it to me shortly after we started having sex. I think initially it was for security reasons, but as I thought more about it, I figured that she just liked suprise's. I felt that she liked the idea of being left in suspense and wondering would I come and lay in the bed with her that night. Every once in a while I would creep into the house without calling or announcing my presence.

Marie would sometimes jokingly say,

"You better call before you come over here; before you mess around and get your feelings hurt."

At that time I knew she was only playing, if she wasn't, I didn't care; it wasn't like she was my girl. Marie and I had an understanding. When we were in each other's company; we would give each other the same respect that we would want in return. When we weren't then, what the other doesn't know won't hurt them. This mainly included just my activities because Marie made it known real soon that she was very interested in me, and that there was no others. I always felt like how was I to know that she was telling the truth?

Marie had seen something in me before I could see it in myself. "A good Man." She wanted us to be together, but she knew that my heart was still with Renee. She would see my car parked over Renee's mother's house. I would also bring Renee and my daughter over my house, which was next door to Marie. At this stage in my life, I was real bold with mine.

During all of this Marie and I weren't claiming to be a couple. We were just enjoying each other's company.

One day, while I was out, I received a call from Renee. She was crying and cursing.

"Who the hell is Marie, Michael?"

What are you talking about Renee?

"You know what I'm talking about, Marie just called me."

She called and said what?

"She told me that you were sleeping with her, and now she's pregnant."

She's what? Oh hell no, Baby dry your eyes, and stop buggin, I will call you right back.

"No don't call me back, I hate you, and I never want to speak to you again."

"Click. "

I sat there for a minute and just gathered my thoughts. My shit has really just hit the fan. Marie told me that she was pregnant a week ago. Renee and I had just started to get back together. I wanted to break it to Renee gradually. I was just so shocked that Marie would stoop to this level. She must have got the number from my pager. I just sat down while all kinds of things just ran through my mind.

I grabbed my cell phone and called Marie.

"Hello" Marie answered.

What the hell is wrong with you?

"What do you mean?"

You know what I mean; you had no right calling Renee and telling her that.

"Somebody had to tell her, since you weren't man enough"

What's that suppose to mean?

"Just like it sounded. You should have told her, and maybe I wouldn't have to."

Marie if you have messed things up for me, and the only woman I have ever loved; I will kill you.

"Whatever punk, I will see you in nine months."

"Click."

Damn, I'm tired of people hanging up on me.

I got in my car and went over Renee's mothers house. As soon as I arrived, her mother answered the door and said Renee doesn't want to speak to you right now. I pleaded with her mother to talk to Renee for me and tell her that I was sorry, but that was useless. I think her mother was a little disappointed in me also. I left the house realizing that this was something that only time could heal.

CHAPTER 13
THE ART INSTITUTE OF PITTSBURGH

After all of the drama that went on between Marie and Renee, I needed a break. It just so happen that the school I was interested in had came to town one weekend. They were signing up students for the winter quarter. I had received brochures in the past and I was pretty interested in the school. I was going to major in Music & Video Production. I stayed for the orientation, and to fill out my financial aid applications.

Both Marie and Renee had stopped speaking to me. Maybe the distance will make Renee and I grow closer to each other. I wasn't seeing any one at this time, so I didn't have to plan any long drawn out goodbyes. I told only my mother and a few friends of my plans.

Four weeks later, I moved out of my house, and packed up my car. I hit the highway by myself and arrived just in time. As soon as I arrived I had to go to administration to finish some last minute paper work. That took almost two hours, and then I was given directions to my apartment. My apartment was in Allegheny Centre, right next to River Front stadium, where both the Steelers, and Pirates play.

I got settled in and called my mother to let her know that all was well. Then I received a call from Chris. Chris was my roommate. He called to let me know that he was still in Chicago visiting with his girlfriend. He said that he would be there in about a week.

Once we got off the phone, I thought that I would drive around and take a look at the city.

I went downtown, because when I came into town, that's where all the people were. There was a band playing in the town center, and there were numerous people shopping in the local stores. This wasn't downtown Brooklyn, but it will do for now.

I stayed downtown and went into a local restaurant, and ordered one of their supposedly famous Steak Hoagies. I should have kept my damn money in my pocket though. The meat was so dry that I felt dehydrated after just one bite. You would think that since Pittsburgh was so close to Philly that they would have their shit together, but that wasn't the case at all. That cook needed his ass beat, and the owner needed to be arrested, for serving something that nasty.

After a few hours walking around, I went back to my apartment. As I was about to go into the door I saw a woman coming out the door who was madd thick. Baby was right, and her gear was proper. I was tired and I just got into town, so I didn't want to make it seem like I was hungry. I figured I would see her again but, if I didn't so what.

I finally made it into the building and up the elevator to my apartment. I went inside and laid right down on the bed. I was too tired to even take my shoes off. I woke up later and went around the corner to do a little grocery shopping. By the time that I made it to the store and back to my apartment it was 9:30 PM. It had just dawned on me that I was supposed to call Renee. So I called and she had company. One of her girlfriends was over her house, and it sounded like a party was going on. I guess they were celebrating my departure. We didn't talk that long because all the commotion was pissing me off. I hung up the phone with her, and called my friend Nesha.

We hadn't spoke in a while, so I thought I would call and see what was going on with her and her family. Nesha's Family was real cool, and her mother loved me. I remember going over there one day. I didn't even call before I came over.

I went to the door and rung the doorbell. Nesha's mother answered the door and said,

"Michael, how have you been? You know I was thinking about you just the other day." After she said that, Nesha came out from the family room smiling.

What's so funny, I asked.

"Nothing, give me a hug"

Why are you talking low?

Do you have company?

"Yeah"

Well who is it?

"My boyfriend is in the family room"

I just laughed for a minute and then I asked Nesha,

You mean to tell me your mother said that she was thinking about me, while your boyfriend was there?

"Yeah, I was like damn she buggin"

She's not buggin, she just loves me, just like her daughter.

"Whatever"

Ok, I'm going to leave. I will call you later.

As soon as I started to walk towards the door Neesha's mother called out,

"Mike I know you're not about to leave already?"

I just laughed for a minute.

Yeah, I'm going to go, but I will keep in touch.

"Ok, don't be no stranger."

I won't.

I left the house and got in my car and just laughed. I would have been really pissed if that was me sitting in there with my girl, and her ex came by, and received that kind of welcome.

The phone rang a couple of times and then Nesha's mother answered.

"Hey Mike how are you? And why haven't you been over here to visit me?"

I'm fine, but I live in Pittsburgh now. I'm out here going to school for Music and Video Production.

"Really? That's good. You take care of yourself and let us know if you need us, here's Neesha."

"Hello"

What's going on?

"Nothing, just chillin"

Were you busy?

"Not really, just sitting in the living room talking with my boyfriend."

Oh well, I won't keep you long, I just wanted to call and see how you were doing. I will call you later.

"Ok, but make sure you call me though"

I will, bye.

Once I got off the phone, I ironed my clothes for my first day of school. I was going to wear my Guess jeans, my navy blue hoody, and my white and navy Nike 1's.

The first day of school was great. I had a lot of fun. I met a few new friends, and got to check out a lot of the equipment that we would be using. I had a friend I started to hang with named Frog. He was madd cool. After school was out, we went back to my apartment to hang out for a while. While Frog was over, I got a call from Renee. We really didn't speak that much, because every little thing that I said, she would remind me that I had a baby on the way, by another woman. She threw the shit in my face on a regular. Who could blame her? I should have played my cards a little better. That day Renee and I talked for a few minutes, but I didn't hold conversation long, on the count that I had company. She just called to see when I wanted her to bring my daughter to see me. I figured that maybe if I could get her out here, she could take a break from everything that was going on in Buffalo. We could both spend some time and talk about us getting back together. She said that she would catch the bus and visit in two weeks. We hung up the phone, and I grabbed my keys to take Frog home. He was living up the hill, with his girlfriend, and his ex lived across the street from them. I was like damn he's bold. I went in the house for a few minutes, and then I went home.

Renee arrived and visited with me for a week. Our visit was a nice one. We went to walk by the lake, and I showed her around my school. I had a lot of fun with both her and my daughter that weekend. Michay was just starting to walk, so she was real busy. But anytime, that I mentioned anything relating to Renee and I getting back together, she would just get upset and start crying. All of my trust was gone. She didn't believe a word that I said. It just made her upset even more, when I mentioned that Marie and I were back speaking. I only told her because I wanted to be honest and share everything with her. I wanted us to make it work this time.

About a week later Renee went back to Buffalo, and I got on with my education. School was great, and I loved being there. It is funny how; once I got away, I was able to look at life a little different. I really analyzed my situation and came to terms, that I was about to be a father a second time. I knew that the only way that I would be able to give my daughters a good life, was if I stayed in school, received my education, and made something of myself.

In May of 1996 I had to go back to Buffalo for sentencing. My case involving Renee's father was not yet over, this was the final stage, and I was facing 3 to 7 years in State Prison if convicted. I packed up all of my stuff at the apartment and told my roommate that I was going home to take care of some family business; and someone in my family may be coming

for my things. Deep down inside I knew that I was going to be sentenced to the maximum amount of time available. I arrived home the night before court, and I spent time with Micay and visited my people's on the block.

The next morning, my mother and I drove down to the court house. I waited outside the courtroom for my lawyer

Sal to show up. About 10 minutes went by and then Sal came and said that he still needed to speak to the judge in his chambers for a minute, and that he would be right out.

Thirty minutes later, Sal walked out of the Judge's Chambers and Judge Mario Rossetti followed him. They called order, and proceeded to call my case. I walked up to the stand and stood at the side of my attorney, and a deputy came and stood on my right. The judge started to speak to me in a loud, but subtle tone.

"Mr. Martin are you still in school? How is that working out?"

Yes Sir, I am. I love school.

"I received many letters, from a lot of very influential people I might add, regarding the fact that you shouldn't go to jail."

I looked him in the eye as he went on.

"Mr. Martin these letters said a lot about your character, but your actions spoke louder. You have made it to all of your necessary court dates, you have been listening to your mother, staying out of trouble, and at the same time you found yourself a job and now you're attending school. You have done all of this, not because you were told, but for your own benefit. Do you have anything left to say before I impose sentencing?"

Yes your honor.

First, I wanted to say that I'm sorry for the crime that I committed, and that I just want to put this whole thing behind me. My crime has caused both of our family's a great deal of pain, both mentally and physically. Now I just want to get on with my life.

He acknowledged my plea with a nod.

"Mr. Martin I sentence you to five years probation, to be served in New York State, but under the supervision of the State of Pennsylvania. You are to report to the proper authorities as soon as you get back in Pittsburgh. Do you understand?"

Yes Sir.

"Well good luck to you Mr. Martin."

Thank You Sir.

I left the courtroom and my mom and I just celebrated and thanked God right there in the hall. I just knew that I was going to jail. I was so convinced that it was over, that I left my wallet, keys and jewelry under my mother's passenger seat. I was the happiest person in the world that day. The next day, I hopped on the bus and went back to school. The day that I returned I was given my first film assignment.

For my filming and editing class, I had to prepare a five minute short. I chose to do a film on the choice that a teen had to make between school and the streets. I entitled the project "Keepin it Real". I had my man, Emery, travel to Pittsburgh to be in the film. When he first came to town, we went downtown to see what we could come up on. There wasn't that much action downtown though, just a lot of lookers. But that's natural especially being with Emery. He thought he was a pretty boy, and he always went out of his way for women. He was starting to piss me off, so we went back to my apartment. A few days later, we started going over my storyboards and making the necessary changes so that we could start filming the next morning.

We had filmed all of the shot's in two days, now the only thing left for me was the editing. I told him that I was going to do that tomorrow. The day after we finished filming, Emery caught the bus home. I went back to my daily school activities and started editing the film.

During my spring break, I began an internship at WBLK in Buffalo. Nesha's father was the program director at the time. I wrote Mr. Faison a letter and shared my career plans with him. He responded, and just told me to notify him of the dates that I was available. As soon as I went home, I immediately began to work at the radio station. During the day, I would assist and learn the business of marketing and promotions. In the evening, I would sit in with DJ Hooker, and Break-a-Dawn, learning the business of production. Chillin with them two at night was madd fun. I was very fortunate to be able to work with them. Hooker is just full of jokes and laughs. He's a little short dark brother. Dawn is a fine ass sister from Brooklyn. She is as sexy as they come. Dawn is a perfect catch, because she has beauty and brains. I was doing my thing at the radio station for about three weeks. Once my internship was over, I went back to school in Pittsburgh. As soon as I got back, with the training that I received at the radio station back home, I was now able to DJ at our school's Radio Station. I was like a kid in a candy store. I was really starting to see myself getting out of Buffalo forever, and making something of my life.

Every time that I began to enjoy school, Renee would call me and accuse me of abandoning her and my daughter and leaving her to raise my daughter alone. I didn't have much, but whatever I had I would give it to her, even if she didn't need it.

Just six months after I had started school, I had to quit. I went home to help raise my daughter. When I got back in town, I started driving taxi again. It was summer and the taxi business wasn't as profitable for me as it has been in the past. So, while I was driving taxi, I started back hustling. I figured this was the life for me. I had given up on school and all of my other hopes and dreams of ever getting out of the hood.

I was also a proud father of another daughter. Marie had a girl a few days after I had came back to town. Her daughter paged me one day, while I was on the block to tell me the news. She just told me that her mother had a girl and that she would be home in a few days, and she would call me then.

I went over to see my newborn daughter Michelle a few days later. She was so small. She looked just like me when I was a baby. Marie and I sat and talked that day about a lot of things, and what we both needed to do for our daughter. I started to go by Marie's house and visit with my daughter a few times out of the week, and sometimes I would take Michay with me. Michay loved seeing her little sister. Every once in a while Marie would let me know that I still had a place in her heart, but not in so many words. It was the little things that she would do, like start cooking around the time that I was coming over. She would always have just enough left over for me.

When I moved back to Buffalo, the rumors about Renee's lifestyle while I was gone were floating around. Everytime that I would approach her about something that I heard, she would just deny it. I would finally come to the realization that in order for me to believe that something was going on, I would have to see it for myself, and that's exactly what I did.

It was a very hot and humid summer day in July of 1996. I had just finished playing basketball in front of Antonio's house, which was next door to where my girlfriend Renee lived. She was not feeling well that day; otherwise I would have been spending time with her. I had been playing basketball for about an hour now, but the heat made it feel more like a lifetime.

I decided to take a much needed water break. I went into Antonio's house to see if he had anymore of that good Kool-Aid his mom's always makes. I walked through the living room, then I paused, due to the noises I was hearing coming from Renee's house next door.

I went into the dining room, and then up to a nearby window, that made Renee's room visible. As I glanced out of the window, all that I could see was a glimpse of someone walking over to the bed. I looked over my shoulder to see if anyone was in my presence, but I was the only witness.

What exactly was I witnessing? I began to ask myself.

It was too dark for me to really see anything going on in Renee's room. Every once in a while, with the glare from a passing car's headlights, I would see movement, but it was brief. From a quick glance at my watch I realize that I have been standing here for almost twenty minutes. There was still no movement visible. All that could be heard were giggles and playful noises.

What are you doing Michael? I immediately began to ask myself.

But I was not able to muster up enough strength to move. By the time that I had concluded that I was not supposed to be there, it was too late. Finally the lights came on in Renee's room.

I grabbed a nearby chair and stood on it, to see if that would enhance my view, and it did, maybe a little too much. Up stood Renee, wearing nothing but that which she came into this world with. Then, my friend Ty stood naked, right next to her.

Michael, why did you stay? I began to ask myself.

I couldn't answer that then, but now the real question that I ask myself now is, why did I keep what I saw that evening to myself all these years?

For a while I would think about approaching her and telling her what I witnessed, but what was the point. We broke up shortly thereafter, but I made up another excuse as to why I didn't want us to be together anymore.

CHAPTER 14
THE BLACKER THE BERRY, THE SWEETER THE JUICE

I had just come from picking up my man Hassani when I met her. As soon as I turned down Comstock Ave, I spotted her. She was about 5ft 7inches, weighting 160 pounds. She was wearing some Guess jeans that showed off her hips. She had a nice pair of black boots on with a top that showed off her tight stomach. Baby had a booty you could sit a drink on. She was looking sexy as hell, and licking the shit out of an ice-cream cone. After seeing all of that I just had to stop.

Can I have some of that?

She tilted the cone towards me and said

"Here, come and get it."

I jumped out the car and stepped right to her.

Hello my name is Michael.

"Hi, I'm Elaine"

Do you live around here?

"Yeah, I am actually on my way home now. I'm running late for work."

I reached in my car and grabbed a pen and a piece of paper to write my number down.

I don't want to hold you up, so take my number and give me a call whenever you're free.

"Ok, I'll do that."

I hopped back into the car and my man was like damn,

"Did you see her ass?"

Hell yeah. Why do you think I stopped? I had to holla at her.

I went back on the block about an hour later, right after I dropped Hassani off at Jay's house. Once I got on the block, everybody was in the yard gambling.

What's the bank?

Jay grabbed the dice and said

"Two-hundred."

Stop it.

Jay shook the dice in his hand and started talking to the bones. The dice rolled out on the pavement, hit the garage, and landed on 4,5,6.

"Pay me nigga" Jay said all excited.

I threw the money on the ground, and I left the yard. I came back down the block and noticed my man T pulling out of his driveway. His sister and his friends were sitting on the porch, so I just went over to sit with them. T's sister name was Kisha. Kisha was real pretty, and she had madd gear. She would wake up and just sit on her porch and look good all day. Everybody would drive by and try to talk to her. I went over there and as usual she had a porch full of mudducks. I never saw Kisha hanging with someone who looked better than her. I guess she had gotten too used, to all of the attention to let that happen.

I sold a few more packages, and then I decided to turn it in. I went around the corner and hopped in my car and went home. Right after I came home from school in Pittsburgh, Renee's mother had moved to Atlanta. She said that she was only visiting, but in the meantime, she needed somebody to stay in her house, while she was away. I would stay there sometimes, when I wasn't spending the night with Marie. Sometimes Renee would come over and chill with me too.

We had started back kicking it, but now, I was not letting any of my other women go. She had to learn that I was through with the games, I was looking for a woman to be with me; a family.

The next day while I was on the block, Elaine paged me at about 2:00 PM. She said that she didn't have to work that day, and she wanted some company. I let her know that I had a few things to take care of and that I would be over there in a few minutes.

I walked back around the corner to my car and grabbed my bike out of the trunk. I figured what the hell, I'll just ride my bike. I stopped over my mother's house to change my clothes. Once I was changed, I called Elaine back to let her know that I was right around the corner; and I would be there in a minute.

I arrived at her home at about 5:00 PM. She was still looking just as good as she was on the day we met. She had on shorts that day and her legs looked so sexy. She introduced me to her roommates, and they looked fine as hell also. They were both Puerto Rican. I was in heaven. I sat down, and asked her what she wanted to do. I had to take care of a few things on the block in a couple of hours, so we couldn't catch a movie; I told her.

We were hungry, so we both decided on Chinese food. The food was delivered about forty-five minutes later. We ate and watched a little bit of TV. I got a good vibe that girlfriend was feeling me because right when I was about to leave, she gave me this really big hug. She squeezed me so tight as if she never wanted to let me go. At that point, the feelings were mutual.

Once I left Elaine's house, I went back on the block and just chilled with the crew for a minute. The block was hot that night, so I knew that I was not going to be out there long. The police kept circling the corner. I later found out that someone got shot earlier, and that was why the police was rolling so hard. I went back around the corner and put my bike back in the trunk, hoped in the car and drove home. I was a little tired anyway.

As soon as I started driving down the street, I got a page from Elaine. I was smiling from ear to ear. Everyone does when that new person that they're interested in starts to show interest. I stopped off at Scottie's Steak House, to get something to eat, and I called Elaine from the payphone.

What's up Boo?

"Oh, I'm Boo now"

Yes, is that a problem?

"Not at all, maybe that's what I want to be."

Say word?

"Word, otherwise I wouldn't be saying so."

Ma, how long are you going to be there?

"Why, you need to call me back?"

Word, I was here waiting on my food to get done, so I thought I would call you.

"Well call me whenever."

No, I 'm going to call you in like five, ten minutes, soon as I get home.

"Ok, do that then."

I went back in the restaurant, grabbed my food and went home. Once I got in the house and fixed me a plate and a glass of Kool-aid, I called Elaine back.

What you doing?

"Nothing, waiting on you to call."

Really, now you're waiting on me?

"No, not like that. You said you were going to call, so I have just been doing some homework and waiting."

Yeah, Elaine was the right one for me. She had no kids, two jobs and she was a full-time college student. It's been a while since I met a woman that wanted more out of life, besides, her hair and nails done, and a nice outfit, just to sit around the house. Even if Elaine did want those things, she had the means to provide them for herself.

"You know I enjoyed spending time with you today?"

So did I, and I hope we can do it again soon.

"Me too"

Real soon.

She laughed and then said

"Ok, point taken."

I'm sorry, I'm just trying to make sure that you know.

"Know what?"

That; I'm very interested in you.

"If I didn't know, I definitely know now."

We talked for just a little while longer because Elaine had to go to work. After one hour we got off the phone. I needed to get some sleep anyway. I woke up in the middle of the night and called Marie. We were back on good terms, so it was cool. It was about 1:00 AM, when I called.

What's up, did I wake you?

"No, I wasn't sleep."

It's 1:00 in the morning, why aren't you sleep?

"Because I couldn't sleep, I had a lot on my mind."

Like what?

"Nothing that you care to hear about."

If she was referring to, me and her having a relationship, then she was right, I didn't want to hear it.

So what's on your mind?

"Michael what do you want? Why did you call?"

I just called to see how you were doing. I'm sorry I made a mistake, it won't happen again.

"You waited till 1:00 in the morning to see how I was doing. Or did you just get finished seeing how Renee was doing, before you called me?"

Well Marie, I see you're buggin tonight, and I guess that's my cue. I'm sorry I bothered you. I will call you later.

"Don't hang up, why are you getting off the phone with me?"

For one it's too late for me to be listening to you run your mouth about stupid shit. For two, you don't know what you're talking about. And I don't even know why you're buggin anyway, you're not my woman and neither is she.

"Oh she isn't?"

Don't even act like I didn't tell you we weren't together.

"You're still sleeping with her."

See, there you go running your mouth about something you don't know; again.

"Whatever Michael, I'm not stupid."

Ok whatever, I'm about to lay it down. I might stop by tomorrow.

"Call before you come nigga."

Once I got off the phone with Marie, I looked over at the clock and it was 2:00 in the morning.

I really wanted to talk to Elaine, but I couldn't call her this late; it was to early in the relationship. I just laid my head down and caught a few more hours of sleep.

CHAPTER 15
BACK ON THE BLOCK

I woke up and got dressed at about 6:00 in the morning. It was the first of the month, and I wanted to be out on the block early. Welfare checks didn't come in the mail anymore, but instead, through this little ATM like debit card. People would wake up as early as possible, and some wouldn't sleep at all. The grocery store, around the way would open at 7:00 AM. I knew that once a few of them got their money, they would be looking to get high. I planned on supplying all their needs. I grabbed my car keys and my bundle, and headed out the house.

I went to McDonalds first. I always felt that you shouldn't hustle on an empty stomach. I ordered my usual that morning; hotcakes and sausage, and a medium coffee. I got my food and headed back to the block. I usually eat breakfast, lunch and dinner around the way, especially on the first because I wasn't trying to miss any money.

That morning the block was empty, but right after I put my bundle in the stash, I seen someone coming down the street. Whoever said drug dealers take the easy way out lied.

Take for example, this gentleman coming down the street. He could be a crack head strung out looking to rob me, an undercover officer, looking to bust me, a stick up kid looking to rob me just on GP.

For the most part, the people that I roll with have tried to get a job, but who's going to settle for $5.00 an hour, when you can make $500.00. With that in mind, there's a price we pay and the risks are much greater; jail or hell is the outlook I faced daily.

The person that I wasn't able to see from a distance was finally closer to me. It was my man Flip. Flip is usually playful and talkative. He's always talking about what he used to have, and what he used to do. Not this morning though, Flip had money and there was only one thing he wanted to talk about; getting high. I gave Flip his packages, and he was on his way. I grabbed my bike out of my trunk and started to ride around. I wanted to see who was out on the other corners as well. I left my bundle in the stash, while I left. I didn't want to get stopped by the "jakes" and I also wasn't about to post up on nobody else's block; that was a "no-no." There were rules to the street and for the most part, I followed them. You're always going to have a few knuckleheads, who just do whatever, but in the end, it catches up with them. I'm out here in the streets, but I'm not of the streets. I'm not a gangster or a killer, and nor do I claim to be. But I have met a few in my time, and I know how they think; they don't. Deep down I have dreams and goals, but in one way or another, this road is one that I must travel to reach my destination. Otherwise, why would God have me out here going through this? These were thought's that went through my mind and the minds of others, who were out in the game with me.

I had been circling the neighborhood while hitting a few licks in between that time. It was now 9:00 AM and a few more people came outside with the same game plan as I had in mind; get money. I wasn't a big time hustler I was just trying to get by. Truthfully, I was just a little more than an outfit hustler. There are a lot of people that are in the game that are just outfit hustler's, they just won't admit it. An outfit hustler, hustles just enough to get the latest Jordan's when they come out, nice fresh gear daily a little bit of jewelry and if he has a car, they want a booming system and some rims on it. They paint this picture like they have it going on, but the truth is that they're really a few dollars away from broke. Many times that lavish lifestyle is what gets them caught up, when they find themselves in somebody's trunk. I like to save money for rainy days, and in my line of work, there were a lot of those. My gear was ok, and I had a little bucket to get around in, so I was straight. I couldn't be an outfit hustler even if I wanted to, because I had two daughters now. Not everyone is an outfit hustler or small time. Actually, most of the people in my crew flip bricks, but you wouldn't know it unless you knew them. They just have a few more outfits than me and maybe a nicer car, but not too nice. You can do your thing, as long as the hater's don't feel you're doing too much. Jay-Z said it best; The Streets are Watching.

At about 11:00am, my man T pulled up in his mother's yard. T was plugging mostly everybody around the way. If they weren't getting it from him, then they were getting it from my man Julio. These boy's sold the big weight. I used to hug the block all day, so no matter what I bought, it was all getting dimed up. I don't care if I coped two Ki's, I would dime that up too. I needed to see all my paper. T went in his mother's house for a minute and came back out and kicked it with me.

"I see you out here trying to get it?"

If I don't, somebody else will.

"You already knowing."

No doubt, but what's up with you? Girlfriend must have put it on you; you're just now coming out.

"You know how it be, you the big playboy around here."

Naw you took my title long ago. But I will tell you this I got a hott joint that I just met a few days ago. I was chillin with her last night for a minute.

"Word? I was wondering where you were last night."

I was chillin, wit baby from Brooklyn. Yo, girlfriend got two jobs and she go to school.

"You better be trying to keep that one, but you know Renee ain't having that."

We both laughed.

Come on man, I deaded that a long time ago. It's over between us.

"Yo why she be buggin like that then?"

Because of the way I put those calfs on my shoulders and look her in the eye while I'm killin it. You betta keep yours close nigga, before she get on the martin diet too.

Besides, Renee knows that I'm driven and I have determination. Deep down, she knows that I won't be here forever, the question is will she be able to leave with me, when I decide to take that trip. That messes with her head.

"Bullshit, your ass is the one messing with her head"

We just started laughing again.

"Feed that shit to them hoes that don't know no better, I'm ya man don't try to play me."

I know dog, but you can't blame a brotha for trying.

"Yo stick around because I want you to roll with me later, we gotta talk."

What time?

"About 3:00."

Ok, well I'm going to bounce in a minute, but I will meet you back here at 3:00.

I went down the block a little further, where I had a car waiting for me. After I hit the lick, my pager started going off; it was Renee. I went down in front of the corner store and called her back from the payphone.

I thought I would play with her a little, so when she answered I said

Yo, Who dis?

"What, now you don't know who be paging you?"

I didn't recognize the number.

"Well that just shows what kind of father you are."

What's that suppose to mean?

"You need to start spending more time with your daughter."

I spend a lot of time with my daughter. It's not like you're always with her. Every time that I call my mother's house she's over there, and your ass is out at a club.

"Whatever, you don't know shit."

I know that it must be the truth because you didn't deny it?

"You only know that I went out because your gay ass friends told you that they saw me."

Well anyway, what do you want?

"I want to do it?"

Do What?

"Look if you don't want to, just say that, because I don't have time to play your games."

What games, you're just upset because I'm not kissing your ass.

"So who are you fucking?"

What do you mean, and why are you talking like that?

"You haven't been calling me lately, so you must be giving it to somebody else."

Look, I explained to you that it was over. Yes, I do have somebody, but it's nothing sexual.

"Whatever, so who is she?"

None of your business, you don't know her. Yo I gotta go.

"You're getting off the phone with me?

Yes, I have to go. I might call you back later.

"You might? Don't, don't do me no favors."

"Click."

I just hung up the receiver at the payphone, and headed back down the block. As I went back down the street, I saw T's sister Kisha sitting on the porch, so I stopped by to chill for a minute.

"What's up Mike? How are you?"

Hey beautiful, I'm chillin, what about you?

"I'm ok, just bored, I hate this town."

What are you doing this weekend?

"Nothing, why what's up?"

I might need you to ride with me over the border.

I would have Kisha ride with me when I was going over the border, so I wouldn't get pulled over by the Canadian officials.

"Well, just let me know, I need to get out anyway."

Alright Ma, tell your brother I will be back in a couple of hours.

I went around the corner got in my car, and pulled off. I was madd tired, so I thought I would go over Marie's house to lay it down. I had just got my key back, and I was praying that she wasn't home. I just wanted to go in the house and get some sleep. I can never get what I pray for, because as soon as I turned the corner, I seen her car sticking out of the driveway. I parked my car around the corner, and walked to the house. Once I got in the house, I went to the fridge, grabbed a soda, and went upstairs. Marie was sitting on the bed talking on the phone.

I kicked off my timbs and said wake me up in two hours please.

"Nigga this ain't no damn motel, and don't be creepin up in here like that. Girl, let me call you back."

She got off the phone with her girlfriend.

Look Marie, don't piss me off. Just wake me up in a couple of hours.

"Are you spending the night with me tonight?"

I don't know, just wake me up, we'll talk about it then.

I went to sleep for about one hour, until I was awaken by my pager. Marie heard it going off and started coming up the stairs.

"Do you need the phone?" She said.

I know where it is if I did. Pass me my boots.

I slipped on my timbs and went back out the door. As I was leaving Marie started to yell.

"I hate your ass, and don't come back here tonight."

I just ignored her and went to my car. I drove down the street and stopped at the corner store to use the payphone. I called the number back, and it was Elaine calling me from work.

"Am I going to see you today?"

Sure, what time?

"Whenever it's convenient for you. I just want to see you."

Well, I have to meet my man real quick, and take care of some business, but as soon as I'm done I will call you.

"Ok make sure you call me boo, I really want to see you."

Ok, I will.

When I got off the phone with Elaine, I went back on the block. I was still tired, so I pulled my car in Anthony's yard, reclined my seat and laid down.

About forty-five minutes later, I woke up from the sound of my man T pulling up bumping the beats. He hit the horn and I signaled for him to give me a few minutes. After I rolled up my windows and locked the doors, I hopped in the car with T, reclined the seat and rolled the windows up; so that my face was barely visible through the tint. He kept his window rolled up the same way. T was cool. He treated everybody the same, money or no money. He had dough, but it didn't matter to him. His friends and family were first, and most important to him.

After we were driving for a minute, T turned the radio down, and asked me.

"What are you doing out here? I thought that you would have stayed in Pittsburgh, and went to school."

T, that's what I wanted to do, but my money wasn't right and Renee was buggin, talking about I abandoned her and my daughter.

"Word, she used to say all that?"

Hell yeah, on a daily bases. She knew how to push my buttons. I came home just to hear about all the shit she was doing while I was away.

"So you just quit school, came back here to this hell hole and now you're not even with her anymore; Damn."

"You don't belong out here. I mean none us do really, but you have too much going for you and I can tell that you don't want to be here."

You are right T, but right now this is the only thing that I have right now. I tried to get a job, but they only want to pay a brotha slave wages. Me and my family gotta eat.

"Do you think I don't know? I been there too, but I realized a long time ago that this was the life for me. Not by choice, but by coincidence. This money started coming too fast, and now that I have been doing it for so long, it's not like I can just go and fill out a job application, telling them that I graduated five years ago, and I never had a job."

I know, because the first thing they're going to ask is what have you been doing since high school?

We had drove around for about an hour just kicking it. The conversation was a good one. Most people on the outside looking in, look down on brotha's that be posting up on the corners. I have come to understand their situation, just like others. Many of the people that I run with hustle because it's there, and there's not much else. They have been doing it so long, that it's all they know. Their attitude is who's going to hire me? And if they do hire me, I can't wear my dreads or I gotta cut my braids, just to make minimum wage and have somebody order me around all day, I don't think so. It's a very sad situation that some of us go through, that hurts even more when there's no one to feel your pain or at least listen to you. After talking to T, I looked at him different. It's one thing to know yourself that you're not happy, but when others point it out, and when they can tell you the same things that have been going through your mind; it's a wake up call.

"Look player, I just wanted to let you know that whatever you need, I got you."

I know that T, and I appreciate it.

"Just think about what I said and decide what you want from life, and go and get it. Don't wait for it to come to you."

T dropped me off and kept going down the street. I got out the car and hollered at my man Boog for a minute. The conversation that T and I had stayed on my mind. Boogie was talking, but I wasn't even hearing what he was saying. I just thought to myself; damn, I gotta get my shit together.

CHAPTER 16
FRIDAY NIGHT

After shopping all day I finally found the perfect "fit" for the evening. There are still a few hours before it's time to get ready, so I'll just go back on the block, to see, who's all going out tonight. The minute that I arrive, I overhear everyone yelling. The crew is trying to convince my man Tory to roll with us tonight. Tory is that one friend whose girl has him on lockdown. That is something that Tory will never admit to, at least not in front of the crew. Boogie on the other hand, swears up and down, that he can come and go as he pleases. The real truth is that, his girl put him out the house two weeks ago for thinking just that. Boogie and his girl Kenya are sickening; they both go out to the same club and dance with people just to make each other jealous. When the club is over, he jumps on the cell phone to argue her down about why she didn't dance with him.

Me myself, I've been a playa since the formation of the Himalayas. At the time I was staying with Marie and Elaine while still messing with Renee on the low. I was also living in Renee's mother's house, while she was away. With Marie there's never really an argument regarding me going out. We have an understanding; I'm grown and I come and go as I please.

I have this feeling that it will just be Boogie and I hanging out tonight.

I was feeling a little tired, so I decided to go home and take a nap. I told Boogie, to call me at the crib when he was ready. While I was getting in my car, he snuck in a wisecrack.

"Goodnight Mike, we'll see you tomorrow. You know Marie don't let you come out after the street lights come on."

I just laughed it off and ignored him because he and I both know the truth.

As soon as I walked in the door I'm greeted by Marie telling me my plate is in the oven.

Through his stomach, is still the way to a man's heart.

Best believe that old saying still holds true.

I sat down and looked over the plate before reciting my grace. My baby prepared a T-bone steak, steamed rice with gravy, and Steamed mixed-vegetables. Before I could finish Marie came down the stairs, gave me a kiss, and poured me some Kool-aid. She made my favorite flavor that night; grape, with slices of lemon in it. I took a sip of the drink, and then I told Marie

I'm going out this evening.

"What else is new?"

It's not even like that

"Whatever, just don't think you're going to be coming in here all times of night."

Yeah ok.

I gave Marie a gentle kiss on the forehead, and then I went upstairs to lie down.

About two hours after I layed down, Marie woke me up because my phone was ringing.

"Answer your damn cell phone or turn it off"

I just layed there and let it ring. Once the phone stopped ringing she started up.

"Was that your girlfriend calling you? Is that why you didn't answer it?"

No, it was Boogie.

"Damn, don't boogie got a damn woman? He call's too much."

I will let him know what you said.

"I don't give a damn, I'll let him know myself."

Whatever.

I figured that Boogie must have been calling to see if I was ready, so I decided to take my shower and get dressed before I called him back. It's Hip-hop night at the club tonight, so timbs, Guess jeans, a wife beater, and my cream Avirex leather will do just fine. I put my glasses on just to tease Marie, and it works.

"Who in the hell are you trying to look good for?"

"Beep" "Beep,"

"Mwua." I kissed her on the cheek

That's Boogie, baby don't wait up.

I went outside and hopped in the car. Boogie had the beat's bangin. He was playing the "One More Chance" remix, by Biggie. That is the perfect song to get a brotha vexed, before a party.

As soon as we hit the parking lot this fine ass sister walked in front of the car. I'm like

damn, baby know she don't have to be that thick."

By this time I'm hyped, like, yo hurry up and let me up in this piece. As soon as we went up in the spot, a few chicken heads that live around the way greeted us. We chilled for a minute before making our way to the bar. Then the DJ put on "Benjamin's" by Puff Daddy, and the crowd went wild. Boogie and I made our way to the dance floor. As soon as we stepped up on stage, we were both, snatched up by two fine ass females. They were both madd thick. I looked over at Boogie to see if he was having as good of a time as I was. By the expression on his face, it was obvious that he was enjoying himself. He was holding up one of Baby-girl's legs, and doing his thing. It was obvious that she wasn't new to this because she was throwing it at him, like what? He looked over at me

" Damn, it's like that?"

He was commenting on the fact that I had my partner bent over grabbing her ankles, while shaking her ass.

I responded with huh playboy, what now?

Then girlfriend turned around and faced me, dancing really seductive. Her hands were under my shirt and all over my chest. Then she showed me her tongue ring. Boogie looked over at me, and at the same time we both said.

"ooh we"

Girlfriend freaked the hell out of me all night. I looked at my watch and it was 3:47 AM. The club closed at 4:00 AM, so I had to make my move. I asked girlfriend that I was dancing with

What's up for the rest of the morning? I know you're not tired?

I didn't wear you out did I?

"Hell no, and by the way, my name is Shay."

Nice to meet you Shay, I'm Michael. Does your man let you come out often looking this good?

"What man?"

So, you're single?

"Yeah a little something like that, I just have friends. Where's your girl?"

I put her to bed before I came out.

"Oh, you got it like that?"

I'm just playing, Shay I don't have a woman, just friends.

The next thing I know, here comes Shay's cockblocking girlfriend with an evil look in her eye.

"Girl is you ready? I have to work tomorrow."

I have been in the game long enough to recognize a hater line. I was a little tired myself, so I just gave Shay my business card. While she's reading the card, I tell her

Don't let none of your men find that.

"They won't, but where is my goodnight hug?"

I gave her a hug, and then we went our separate way.

As soon as we got in the car Boogie was like

"What happened wit oh girl? I thought you and baby girl was going to the telly."

Her friend was buggin, so I was like goodnight.

I was tired from all of the dancing, so I fell asleep as soon as I got in the car. Boogie woke me up, when we pulled up in front of Marie's house.

Yo, I'll see you on the block tomorrow.

"Word, One"

I went in the house, and straight to the fridge, to get a glass of Kool-aid. I filled up my glass and headed up the stairs, to the bedroom. Marie was lying there naked, like she's knocked out. I took off my clothes and slid under the sheets. I started caressing her body, and then I said

Come here boo.

She moved closer saying,

"Which one of them young girls got you all worked up tonight?"

I don't know what you're talking about. I just wanted to be with my Boo.

I got out of the bed and put Jodeci's latest CD in the changer. I slid back in bed and proceeded to try and put the headboard through the wall. Marie and I went at it for like an hour. Afterwards I got up, and went to the bathroom to pay a long overdue water bill. As soon as I came back to the bedroom, Marie was lying there, sleeping like a baby. I slid back under the covers, and kissed her on her neck and her cheek. I gave her one last kiss then I put my arm around her

and told her goodnight.

CHAPTER 17
CAUGHT OUT THERE

Elaine and I had been dating for a minute. I broke everything off with both Marie and Renee. I would still wake up early in the morning to take Renee to work though. Elaine and I had a real cool relationship, and what she didn't know didn't hurt her. Renee didn't want me back in her life until she noticed my relationship with Elaine was growing.

One morning, while I was with Elaine, I received a page from Renee. When I called back we talked for a while, but I cut the conversation short. A few seconds later Renee pressed *69 and called right back. Elaine's roommate answered the phone and then came into our room and said there's some woman named Renee on the phone for Michael. As soon as I got on the phone, she was all histerical.

"I know you don't have a bitch in my mothers house?"

No, I'm not at your mother's house. I'm over my girl's house.

"Your girl? Oh now you got a girl?"

You know I told you about Elaine, and anyway I'm sleep.

"Well you and that bitch stay right there because I'm on my way."

Ok, we'll see you when you get here.

"Click"

I just layed back down and went to sleep. This was at the time that I was still house-sitting for Renee's mother, and Renee thought we were over there. She was too dumb to realize that she pressed *69. She honestly thought that she dialed her mother's number and we were over there. I was tired of playing her games, so I just let her believe whatever she wanted to. I woke up a few hours later and Jay came to pick me up.

As soon as we were pulling up to her mother's house, Renee was pulling away from the house in a taxi. When I stepped out the car I noticed that the front porch window was broken out.

Damn this dumb broad done went on a rampage.

When we walked in the house, my clothes were tore up and they were everywhere. She cut up everything that I owned. A few minutes later she came storming into the house with a butcher knife chasing me and threatening to kill me.

"Why did you and Jay take the bitch home?"

Look dummy, We just got here.

"You're going to lie to my face now?"

"Slash"

She cut me across my elbow.

What the hell is wrong with you, are you crazy?

"I sure am, and I'm about to kill your ass in here today."

"Slash"

She cut me across my arm.

Yo Jay grab this crazy ass broad.

"Renee, why you buggin, I just picked Michael up, nobody was here."

"You're his friend I know you would lie for him."

"Beep" "Beep"

Renee's taxi was blowing the horn.

"You're lucky, I have to go now, but I'm going to see your ass later."

Whatever, I'm calling the police, I'm tired of this. Look what you did to my clothes.

"Blame it on that bitch you were sneaking around with; Bye."

I was lying there bleeding, trying to get a towel to stop the blood. Jay just walked around the house like damn. Then he asked me

"Yo what's wrong with her, why she be buggin like that?"

because she's crazy, she has lost her damn mind.

"What do you be doing to woman? I don't know anyone else who has these kinds of problems."

Whatever man all I know is this dumb broad really thought I was here and cut up all my stuff.

"Damn you're lucky that you didn't have anybody here, or yaw would both be dead."

Shit I doubt that, Elaine is from Brooklyn she be representin, she would have whipped Renee's ass.

"Yeah because Renee only weights like 115 pounds."

See, you know Elaine would have won.

"Well Yo are you going to be ok, because I have to go to work."

Word, I'm alright, I'm just going to clean up and grab what things I have left and go back over Elaine's house.

"Just get up wit me later then."

Alright, One.

Renee and I didn't speak for a while after that incident. Elaine held me down and bought me some new outfits, and so did Marie.

Elaine was right for me I could feel it. She continued with school and kept both of her jobs. We were together for about three months, and then I got that page.

Yo what's the deal Ma?

"When are you coming home because we need to talk."

Talk about what?

"Just when are you coming home?"

I don't know I hadn't planned on coming for a while.

"Well can you come sooner?"

How soon?

"Like now."

I'll be there in a minute.

I chilled for a little while, and then I went home to see what she wanted. As soon as I came in the door, she greeted me with a kiss and we both sat down.

"My thing never came."

What, you needed me to help you look for it?

"I'm talking about my period."

Oh, that thing. How late are you?

"Real late, I'm pregnant."

How do you know that?

"Because I took a pregnancy test."

If you took a pregnancy test and it came back positive, what the hell are you worried about a period for?

"I'm not I just wanted to let you know to see what you would say."

We talked for a long time that evening and I really felt bad. I should have been more careful. Elaine had goals, and dreams, she wasn't a hoodrat, like some other people I knew. I felt that I ruined her life.

After a few months Elaine started acting pregnant, and buggin. I had started staying some nights with Marie. Marie was always there, it was like she was just waiting for me to come around. That time wasn't coming anytime soon though. I used to also kick it with Renee. She had graduated from this training program my mother got her enrolled in, and now she was working, trying to move out into a nicer area. We would kick it and go out from time to time, but she was still a bitch, and it would always come out.

CHAPTER 18
ALL THE DETAILS

I was tired of working for people. I felt that I was born to be an Entrepreneur. In April of 1997, I started my own business. At the time that I started All the Details, Renee and I were back together. She was really supportive and our relationship was a lot better.

When I first started out, my place of business was inside my mother's garage. I had stopped hustling, and spent all of my money on supplies. I received a lot of support from my crew, and everyone else from around the way. I was so happy to be taking this giant step, but I didn't go at it alone. I submerged myself in many books about business. And for the following spring semester, I enrolled in Dyouville College business program.

Initially, business was really slow. I wasn't making that much money, and what I had saved was slowly deteriorating. It came to a point when Renee was taking care of our daughter, the business, and me. She's the type of person that always has to keep reminding you of the things that she has done.

While business was slow, I took on a job at Earl Schieb. I sanded and prepped cars for painting. I also worked a few jobs that I was sent on from a temp agency. I wanted my business to succeed, without the involvement of drugs. I had several friends that wanted to invest in All the Details. Sure the money would have been nice, and it would have taken my business to a new level. But how long was the ride going to last, before the feds shut us down? That was a risk that I was not willing to take, so I had to struggle for a minute.

As I mentioned before, my earlier customers were my peoples from off the block, family members and a few referrals. All of my customers told someone else about my business, which helped increase profits. It still wasn't enough for me to support my family. When I wasn't detailing a car, I was passing out flyers.

A few months had passed and my relationship with Renee wasn't really working out. I finally made that commitment to her, and had become the man that every woman wanted, and she still wasn't satisfied. I rushed home from work, because I had to pick up our daughter from day care. My daughter and I would go home and make a snack, and then take a nap. Once I woke up, I would start making dinner. Then I would feed my daughter and give her a bath.

I would do the laundry and iron the clothes. I would put a plate in the oven for Renee, and run her bathwater. After all of that you know what she would do? She would come home and say she already ate, and she just wanted to go to bed.

This time I told myself, this is the last straw. If our relationship didn't work this time it wouldn't be my fault. I also told myself that this was it, it was either now or never. I was tired of stressing myself out over this woman.

I wasn't getting any mental or emotional support from Renee. The only one that I could talk to was Michayla, at times even that was impossible. She would "shuuush" me, when Barney was on TV. When I tried to talk to Renee about her actions, She told me that I was now feeling what she felt for so many years, but was I really this bad? Now that I think about it, I was worse. I felt that it was God giving me a taste of my own medicine. But damn did it have to be such a powerful dose.

I decided to reach out to someone else for that much needed companionship. I started talking with Elaine and Marie more and more. I would tell them about what I was going through. Mary was much older and wiser, so she shared the truth with me. She used to tell me that Renee, wasn't ready to be loved by me. She was still a little girl running scared. And no matter what I did, it would go unnoticed, until she was ready to make the changes.

Elaine was still a little bitter towards Renee, but tried not to show it. Right before Elaine gave birth to my daughter Armani, I told her that I was in love with Renee and I wanted to be with her. I think that was one of the most honest days of my life. What I said to Elaine that day really hurt her. Deep down inside I feel it stuck with her for a really long time. Since Elaine was back speaking to me and expressing the pain and the hurt that I caused her. I felt that it was the same pain that I was receiving from Renee. Karma is a mutha. Elaine didn't live far from where Renee and I moved. Gradually I began to visit her and my child and before long, we were back on good terms.

I now think about some of the crazy things that I did for Renee, and the one that stuck with me the most is that I sacrificed communication, with my other daughter's mothers, just to stroke Renee's ego. She felt that I could not be trusted. And with my track record thus far, I couldn't blame her.

One day, my man Boogie called me and invited me out to a club the following weekend. I had also stopped going out, to show Renee, I was serious about us, but I was tired of being Mr. Nice Guy. I told Renee my plans for the weekend. Her response was that if I went out that night, then don't come back to her house. That night, after I left the club. I went by the house to see if she would let me in. I knocked on the door; I still hadn't proven myself worthy of my own key yet. I told Boogie to wait while I knocked again. A couple of minutes went by and I got back in the car and said

Take me over Marie's house.

"Damn player, too many to decide?"

Hell no they all just have good qualities.

We both just laughed.

I called Marie from Boogie's cell phone and told her what happened, and that I was on my way. When I got over there, she had come down and let me in. As soon as I walked in the door she told me that she wasn't about to play this back and forth shit. The next day, I got up early and went and moved my stuff out of Renee's house for the last time.

Later that day, while I was on the block with Boogie, a gentleman named Michael called me. He said that he remembered me passing him an All The Details flyer, and was I still in business? When I told him that I was still in business, he asked me if I would be interested in detailing one of his cars. Boogie dropped me off up there about 10 minutes later.

When I got there, he showed me the car that he wanted detailed. It was a 1993 Cadillac Coupe Deville. The exterior was burgundy, with white leather interior. I took it home and cleaned that car, like it belonged to Jesus Christ. When I was done, you could eat off of it. I drove it back up to the dealership.

Michael was pleased. He asked if I would work for him, but I immediately turned him down. I liked being independent, and even if business was slow, it was mine. I didn't want to work for him and receive eight dollars an hour; when I could remain in business for myself and still charge $80.00 a car for detailing. It took me about 3 to 5 hours to detail a car. So working for him I would have been cheating myself.

We both decided on an arrangement that made us both happy. I would detail his cars and use one of the bays at his dealership; in return I provided a discounted rate for his cars. Michael owned three different car lots. He also had a lot of friends in the car business. Meeting him was truly a blessing.

After a while I was starting to feel that I wasn't independent anymore. I was turning down details from my boys off the block, who helped build my business initially. I was no longer washing cars either. I felt that if my customer wasn't paying for a full detail, then I didn't have time for anything else. I was only working on Michaels cars, and in a way, I became dependent on his business.

One evening before leaving the shop I voiced my feelings to Michael. I told him that I think it would be better if I go back to my mother's garage. That way I could still continue to get business from my old customers. We talked for a while and he understood where I was coming from. He offered me the deal of a lifetime. I would continue to detail cars for him and my other customers; at another shop that he owned, but was vacant. This garage was nice. I could fit five cars in the shop area. We worked out a lease agreement later that week, and the rest is history.

I was detailing five to ten cars a day. A few weeks after I moved in I received my new business license with my new address on it. One of the greatest feelings was when I hung my certificate of business on the wall that day. I expanded my business and started selling alarms, car stereos, and custom-rims. Business was great. During this time, I didn't have a relationship with anyone. I stayed with both Renee and Marie from time to time. And I visited Elaine also, but everyone knew that my main focus was All the Details.

My classes at Dyouville were going great. In my business class, the teacher often called on me, since I was already out there making it happen. I didn't mind sharing my experience with the class either.

September had rolled around and business began to decline. I wasn't detailing cars that often and my product sales had slowed down also. After a few weeks into the month of October, I had to move back into my mother's garage, and go back into the workforce

CHAPTER 19
I'M GOING TO BE AN ACTOR

I was really being stressed out. I was living with Elaine, but spending some nights with Marie. Renee wasn't in the picture because she had a new man. I could tolerate Marie the longest, but she had issues, like everyone else. Elaine on the other hand, I had my car registered in her name. When things weren't going so well between us she would threaten to cancel my registration. She knew I couldn't afford the insurance if the car was in my name. During this time I was like a "yo yo", going back and forth, trying to make everyone happy.

After business came to a halt, I started working in a warehouse, on third shift. I kept catching a cold due to loading the truck on a open dock all night. I remained on that job for about two months, and then I got a new one at M&T Bank. I was tired of being bounced around, trying to make ends meet. I started to ask myself what did I really want from life? I often dreamt of being in the entertainment business, but why couldn't that dream become reality? I immediately started going to the library and bookstores to gather as much information as I could. I signed up with local drama clubs, and registered with several local modeling agencies. I signed with my first agent in January of 1998. At the time my agent was promoting me for print modeling. I did some work with a couple of photographers, but I wasn't happy. I was a nervous wreck.

Modeling was too much work. I had to get my haircut once a week, and get manicures. All of that was too expensive for me. I wanted to perform, but not with modeling, I just stood there. I wanted to make people laugh, cry, and smile.

I wanted to be an Actor.

As soon as I voiced this to my agent I sensed that she was not pleased. Two weeks later I seen her for the last time. We both went our separate ways and she wished me the best of luck.

I began sending photos and resumes to several playhouses. Finally, one day I received a call from a director, who was looking for actors, to be in his play. I auditioned and got a part playing Judge Clarence Thomas. It was a low budget play and at times it seemed like there wasn't going to be a play at all. My instincts were right. I went to rehearsal one day, and it was cancelled and the next one was to be announced. At first, it was like every door that I knock on closed in my face.

I decided to voice what I wanted from life to the only person who could give it to me; God.

I began going to church regularly with my mother and I later joined First Shiloh Baptist Church. My relationship with God was beginning to grow, and many different doors started to open for me. I branched out and started submitting my photo's to other talent agencies across the U.S. I received calls from several agents in California, telling me to let them know when I was in town.

Only people who were close to me knew that I wanted to act. Most of the people who got wind of the idea, just laughed. Even Renee laughed at the idea. It was obvious that I was not going to get anywhere in Buffalo, with so many negative people trying to bring me down.

One day while I was standing on the block, I told my whole crew that I was moving to California. The initial response that I received was,

"Yeah right, you'll be back."

"Why do you want to go down there, they killed Biggie?"

I knew that the only way I was going to make believers out of them was to show them. I told my daughter's mothers, that I was leaving also. The response I received from them was the same. What about your daughter's? That was the hardest part of leaving, and it still is whenever I visit. When it came to my daughters, I felt that if I stay, I would either be dead or in jail. The major company's and jobs left Buffalo a long time ago. The only people left there did tele-marketing work, worked at GM, Ford, the bank, or sold drugs. Some held those jobs, and still sold dope. I felt that I wasn't able to offer my daughters anything if I stayed. I was determined to see if I had what it takes to make it in Hollywood. Rather than go through life, I wanted to get from life. I wanted to be able to grow old and say, yes, I did that. Instead of saying what I wish I had done. And that would be the best way that I could teach my kids; by example.

I called my aunt, who lived in Rialto, CA, told her my plans and asked if I could stay with her for a while. We worked out the details and she stated what would be required of me. I began getting ready to leave. All of my friends at M&T were happy for me. A lot of people surprised me and started showing a great deal of support. It was the people who I expected the love and the support from that showed none.

At first I was going to drive, but those plans were, stopped by Elaine. One day while I was sleep over Marie's house, Renee came over there blowing her car horn, for me to come out. This was nothing new, she had gotten bold and started popping up all times of night blowing the car horn for me. That day she said that she just stopped, cause she noticed my car.

"Oh, so you're back with her?"

No, I'm just watching my daughter, while she took care of some business.

"So when are you coming home?"

When you ask your man, and he says it's ok.

"I put him out."

Well you better get him back.

"Why I know you're not still trying to pursue this pipe dream and go to California."

I sure am, and I will be 3,500 miles away from your tired stankin ass.

"Boom"

I slammed her car door and went into the house.

Marie pulled up not to long after that and I left right out. I went around the corner to see who was out on the block. I pulled up and was double parked in the street, when Boogie said

"Where's your license plates?"

What are you talking about.

"You don't have any license plates on your car Dog."

Boogie, I'm tired, and it has been a long day. Don't play wit me man.

"Get out the car and see for yourself."

Sure as my name is Michael, that crazy broad Elaine came and took the license plates off my car.

"Damn, how long was you driving around like that?"

For like an hour.

"If you would have got pulled over, it would have been over."

Yup, it would have been over for her to, somebody would have had to pay her a visit.

I was pissed and everyone on the block stopped laughing because they could see it. I called Elaine.

Yo, what the hell is your problem? Why did you take my plates?

"You should have been home where you belong."

Home? You got it mixed up. That's just one of my spots.

"And that's why your ass ain't got no plates, because you were chillin at your spot."

You took them while I was at Marie's house?

"Hell yeah, now lets see you drive to California with no plates."

Oh, so you're just trying to do whatever you can to keep me here?

"No, I can care less where you go, but you won't be going with these plates."

I hate your ass.

"CLICK"

I hung up the phone.

Yo Boog, follow me over my mother's house, so I can put my car in the garage.

"You ready now?"

Yeah, before I go over here and kill this broad.

We both go in our cars and drove off. Boogie followed me closely, just in case the police wanted to act up. When we got to my mother's house I told her what went down and she just said the usual; I told you so. I was still pissed, so I didn't talk with her to long, she had a way at pushing my buttons. I hopped in the car with Boogie and that was one of the day's I will never forget. While we were driving back around the way, Boogie just came out and said.

"She don't want you to leave, and she thinks she stopped you."

I know dog, misery loves company.

"Listen, stay focused on what you need to do, and whatever you need to get you there, I got you."

I just looked at him for a minute, while he just reiterated.

"Don't worry about nothing."

From that moment on, I just ignored everything that was happening to me and I put all of my energy into getting ready to leave.

On April 14, 1998, I moved to CA, to further pursue my acting career.

CHAPTER 20
WEST SIDE

The night before I left, I visited all of my daughters. Easter was right around the corner, and I had bought a few things for them. When I visited Michelle, Marie wouldn't let me in. She was upset about me leaving. Elaine was cool about the whole thing, because her and I were considered a couple at the time.

I went to Michays house at about 10:00 that night. Renee answered the door, wearing a teddy. She opened the door and stood there and said

"You're really leaving?"

Yes, what did you think it was a joke?

"Yes, as a matter of fact I did, you always talked about leaving, but you never made any attempts."

Well tomorrow isn't promised to me, and I need to do this for me.

"Well your daughter is sleep, I tried to keep her up, but she fell asleep about a half an hour ago."

I walked into Michay's room, and she was just lying there on the bed, knocked out. I sat down on the bed right next to her and tried to wake her up, but she was not budging. I gave her a gentle kiss on the forehead and left the room.

I will call her during my layover tomorrow.

"Ok, have a safe trip and good luck to you."

I got on the elevator, and went back over Elaine's house for a minute.

The next day, when I called Michay from the Houston airport, Renee answered the phone crying. She told me that after I left last night she got in the bed and her boyfriend asked her did she kiss me. She said no. Then he asked her if she wanted to, and she said yes. Then he asked her why she didn't give me a kiss. She said

"I got out of bed and took the stairs down to the lobby to see if you was there, to tell you I love you, and to give you a kiss, but you were already gone.

You ran after me at 11:00 PM with a teddy on? What did your boyfriend say when you came back to the apartment.

"He didn't say anything, and I put him out this morning."

Why did you put him out?

"Because I told him that you and I were going to be together, and I was moving to California."

Are you crazy? You have had different men in your life for about a year now, and now you mean to tell me that you have all of these feelings for me?

"Yes, I do and you used to tell me that we were going to California as a family."

That was before Michay was even born. You have been living with this man for about six months. So, I was just supposed to come over there and tell you to get your things together because we're moving to Cali?

"Yes, and I would have packed them. How could you just leave me?"

She was still crying the whole time, but her last line made me laugh so loud.

You are really bugging, where's your man?

"Did you think I was joking, I told you that I put him out."

Well, first, stop crying and second, I am going to have to call you when I get to my aunt's house. My plane is boarding.

The first day that I was in town, I just relaxed. But the next day, I went to get a membership at the local gym and I applied for several jobs. I woke up every morning at 6:00AM to run and exercise. I would come home from the gym at about 8:30, take a nap and go out and fill out job applications until 12:00 noon. You're taken serious when you take care of business that way; early in the morning.

Renee used to call me from work, to see how I was doing and to talk about her and I getting back together. I used to tell her that I'm in California to stay, and that her and I could never be together. She would just tell me to give her another chance, and that we were meant to be. After a while the phone calls were getting out of hand. She went back to the old Renee; living in the past. She talked about what I did to her during our relationship, and all the pain that I caused her. It was always only about her. One day, I just couldn't take it anymore.

Renee, why are you calling me?

"Now you don't want me to call anymore?"

No, I don't, you have no reason to, we are over, I have moved on with my life, and I suggest that you do the same. Life isn't about going backwards, and I'm never going back to you.

"Oh, now you wanna act stank because you're in California, fuck you."

"Click.".

When Sunday came around we all went to church. My auntie was a member at LIFE, in Rubidoux, CA. The pastor and founder was Pastor Ron Gibson. He was real down to earth in his messege. He was also a good teacher. He really knew the word, and he would put it in a way that made you want to walk in God's path. I joined as soon as the door's of the church was open. My mother always told me "Only what you do for Christ will last." And he was going to be the only one who would ultimately determine whether I would make it or fail in Cali. I went to Church every Sunday and bible study on Wednesday's. I was also told that in order to really be in good shape, you must take care of your body mentally, physically, and spiritually.

Three days after I came to town I received a call from this marketing firm. They invited me in for an interview that day, and hired me on the spot. I had to show up for work the next day. When I arrived they ran me through the routine, as soon as he was done, I knew it was a scam. It was one big telemarketing scam, and I wasn't playing. I went into the superviser's office and told him that the job wasn't for me.

I went home and thought up a few more ideas on what I could do for work. I needed a job otherwise the only thing I would have been acting in is the feature film;

"I am a Bum," starring Me.

That was a role that I had to pass on, so I had to find work. I spent a lot of time at the malls. When the world gives you lemons, go shopping. That's my motto. I began to notice that everyone wore the same thing. Coordination wasn't factored in at all, when most Californian's got dressed. Another Cali downfall was the fact that you had to wait forever and a day for new music to drop. Aside from the movie scene, I felt that California was slow and country as hell.

It was cool though because me and my people's could come out here and not have the worries that we have in NY. For instance, you could come out your house in the morning and not worry about someone waiting in your bushes to stick you. Or, someone telling you where your kids go to school, and threatening their lives, unless you pay up. What about the businessmen, who get taxed every week, by someone other than Uncle Sam? I dare you not to pay up. Living in Rialto, I didn't have those worries any longer. However, you did have gangs. When I think of gangs, I think of more people to turn states evidence, and snitch on you when something goes down.

Cali is the place that commercialized "Drive By's".. It's a coward's way of showing the rest of the low lives that he runs with, that he's hard. He has shot up the whole block killing a couple of people and wounding many, but none of them are the intended target.

And what does the individual that they missed do? He retaliates, doing the same thing as his rival, killing only innocent by-standers. All this is attributed to the colors red and blue, and if that's not the dumbest thing to die or go to jail for then I don't know what is. I guess I had to have lived here my whole life to understand. You don't hear about to many fights in Cali, because as soon as they get started, somebody's running to get their gun. It's easy to pull out a gun. The hard part comes when the barrels pointed at you. I've been on both sides of the barrel, many times throughout my life and it is no picnic at either position.

To keep me busy and put a few dollars in my pocket, I started my own business. MMJ's Hip Hop Spot. I got the proper permits and licenses, and sold whatever I could get my hands on. Clothing for men and women, mix-tapes, books and magazines. I had left my car back in NY, so I used my aunt's van sometimes or I rode the bus. I used to go down to LA and spend my whole day there in the garment district. I was there trying to see the latest trends, and take notice on some of the marketing techniques used.

I had madd free time, so I started to do a lot of reading. The first book that I bought was Think and Grow Rich by Napoleon Hill. That was a good book. It changed my entire outlook on life. I would read it then start reading it again. It seemed like every time that I read it, I learned something new.

I bought a VW Jetta from my auntie's friends, and off to Hollywood I was. I would go as soon as I was finished working out. Right after I had bought the car, only a month later Hollywood was once again put on hold because my clutch went out. When I took it to the shop I had them give the whole car a complete look-over. They returned with a $1200.00 estimate. I left it there and worked something out with the shop owner, where I would pay a little each week.

The same day that my car went bad on me, I received a call from the Burger King around the corner from me. I went to the interview and was hired on the spot. I started work that following Monday, as an evening maintenance person.

CHAPTER 21
WUT UP CUZ?

From day one I hated my job at Burger King, but I kept it because it brought in money that I was able to invest in MMJ's. I went to work, did my job and kept to myself. I was only there to get paid, and at that point in time Burger King was very convenient for me.

One day, I went to work a little earlier than usual. I sat in the break-room, until it was time for me to start my shift. Once I clocked in, I began to wash all the dishes from the morning shift. After I was finish washing the dishes, I started gathering the trash throughout the restaurant. When I came back to the kitchen, the cashiers were yelling back orders, but I wasn't working in the kitchen at the time. A few minutes later, my manager asked me if I could help out in the kitchen, so that we could get caught up. I agreed and started to prepare a whopper with no onions. When I was done, I placed it on the Whopper tray. This guy Jeremy, who I knew didn't like me, starts yelling at me,

"Is this the one with no onion?"

Yeah

"Well next time label the shit."

I immediately stopped what I was doing.

Excuse me?

"You heard me, I said label the shit next time. Why, what's up cuz?"

He was talking while coming towards me.

Look I ain't even that dude, you don't want these problems.

"Fuck you, Cuz."

I faked with the left, and threw a straight right. Before I could finish him off with a left hook, he was already floored from the first punch. As he fell he grabbed my hands as I was trying to finish him off. My manager and another worker grabbed me off of him, and he got up huffing and puffing like he was going to do something. I sat in the break-room as my manager called the police. While I was sitting there, I just kept shaking my head. I was so upset at myself for losing my cool like that, but I was tired of his mouth, and all that trash he was talking. He was walking towards me, and I thought he was going to try something, so I swung first. He slept on me because I was so quiet, but I suspect that he will think wisely about doing it again. I'm not even that beefing dude, but I will bring it if I feel that my life is being threatened.

The police came about fifteen minutes later, asking questions and getting both sides of the story. Then they searched me and put the handcuffs on me. They took me out the back door, and placed me in the police car. I remained silent right after they read me my rights. We went to the Rialto Police Station, and I was asked to tell my side of the story once more. I started telling the officer the story, and she paused me when I mentioned the time when he grabbed my hands.

She radioed to another officer who was at the scene to tell him about Jeremy grabbing me. Then she said that he's going to be arrested also, unless I didn't want to press any charges. The other officer radioed back saying that Jeremy was willing to forget the whole thing as long as I don't press any charges. I was like sure, whatever. This was all new to me. The police was actually working by the book. Back in NY, two people just beef, get up and go home afterwards. If the police do show up it's usually just to break it up, they have better things to do besides fill out paperwork for a fistfight.

The officer took the cuffs off me and let me out through the side door. She offered me a ride back to my aunt's house, but that's not the kind of car I liked riding in, so I passed. When I got home I told my auntie that I had a little altercation at work, and she never asked any further questions.

That evening, I received a call from my mother. She told me that my father had called the family, and he left his number for you to call him. This was wonderful news to me because I hadn't had a conversation with my father in over seven years. My dad had left Buffalo in 1993 and never told anybody where he was going or when he was coming back. I called him as soon as I hung up the phone with my mother.

Hello, Hi dad.

"Hey son, how are you?"

I'm ok, I'm in California now.

"Yeah, your grandmother told me. What are you doing down there?"

I came out here to break in to the acting business, and to get away from the streets of NY. I was really falling off Pops.

"I know Mike. I've been there myself. That's why I decided to up and leave."

So where are you?

"I'm in Pittsburgh, working with this construction company. We design and build assembly plants for large corporations."

We went at it like old friends, getting reacquainted. It felt good to hear my fathers' voice. I told him all about his three granddaughters that he had. And how I had been selling drugs, playing women, and it all just caught up with me. He began to tell me his story, and it sounded just like mine. He said that he was stressed and fed up with all the games that he played, and the mistakes that he had made, and he just needed to get away and be alone. I knew just what he meant by that because I too felt the same way.

Pastor Ron had just recently preached to us about how we have to break the cycle of bad habits that we have received from our parents. I realized while I was conversing with my father that it was all of God's doing. God was showing me a different route. And he was showing it to me a lot sooner than he had shown my dad.

"Michael, I never stopped loving any of yaw for one minute."

I know dad, you just needed some time for you, just like I needed some time for me.

"Are you mad at me? Tell the truth."

For a long time I was, I hated you Pops. However, since we had this conversation, I see what you have gone through, and what you're still going through, and that takes a strong man to endure that. It's not easy for me to be away from my daughters. Many days I cry, but I know that one day it will all be worth it.

"Michael, I'm so glad that you called and we had this conversation. I have to get up for work early tomorrow, so give me a call tomorrow night, and we'll finish."

We hung up the phone and at that moment I felt that a weight had been lifted off of me. I realized that every road that I traveled, my father had already taken. I was pleased to know that he didn't leave because of me, but because of all the woman, the streets, and the games had just taken a toll on him like they had on me.

I broke the cycle. I was so proud of myself for being able to get out while I still had a chance to make something with my life. I didn't call my father the next day, but I did write him a letter that night. I sent him pictures of me and my daughters. I called about a week later, and he had moved.

If I was younger it might have hurt me, but now that I was older, and after the conversation that we had, I just said a prayer and I asked God to keep him safe.

CHAPTER 22
MY FIRST VISIT BACK HOME

The first time that I went back home to visit it was real cool. I really didn't want to come, because I was just starting to make contacts in the entertainment business. When I went home, I was planning on asking Elaine to marry me, but I put it on hold and just watched her behavior for a few days. Elaine and I used to speak on the phone and write to each other daily.

Renee and I didn't speak that much, she had new man and she was really starting to get her life together. I would always ask everyone how Renee was doing though. I was pleased at the response that I received every time. I always told Renee that she could do magnificent things, if she put her mind to it. Maybe my leaving or our last conversation had something to do with her deciding to turn her life around. Deep down inside, she's a good woman and it was hard for me to let her go.

Marie had a man also and we only talked occasionally, whenever I would call my daughter. From time to time, Marie would tell me that she never stopped loving me, but it went in one ear and right out the other. Elaine and I talked about her and Armani coming to join me in California. She had met a few new friends since I left, and was spending a lot of time away from home. I didn't mind though because I felt that I could trust her.

I was making mental notes to myself about whether I should settle down, and Elaine was my number one candidate. I hadn't really met any women in California yet, and besides, I was too focused on getting my body in shape and working on my acting career.

As soon as I came into town, my daughter, Michay, met me at the airport and jumped right into my arms. She and I spent a lot of time together while I was home. I also went to pick up Michelle and Armani, so that they could all play together. When I wasn't with them, I was spending time on the block with my people's or up at Mike's with Jay.

My man T had got knocked since I left, and there was tension in the air. Somehow my man T was convinced that someone in the crew snitched on him. At first, I wondered why would he think that something like that would happen. The more that he told me the story, the moreI realized that someone had fed him some lies.

When someone gets arrested for the first time, the shock has that person thinking of every possible place to lay the blame except where it should be; on them. Mistakes are made every day, and in many instances, they are made for a reason. God never gives us more than we can handle.

Someone from a third party had told T that his man had set him up. T started to believe that it was true. I tried to tell him that how could that be you both are day one people's. Don't believe that or at least hear your man out. My attitude towards the whole thing was this T and I wasn't day one people's, but we became tight as hell.

When I met him, T had an immediate crew that came first. They were boys for many years, so why throw all of that away without a word to one another. Anything can be discussed especially amongst true friends, and if not, it should create a question as to whether they ever friends to begin with?

Friend's are too hard to find these days, so I cherish the ones that I have. I loved T and the rest of the crew with all of my heart, but if we were going to remain friends, there had to be trust, communication, and respect between us. Those are all words that break up most crews, because they lack those principles, but we must prevail.

If there ever comes a time in the friendship when you feel that you can no longer call on your main man; even if it is just to clarify rumors, then you never were friends to begin with. I felt so hurt that part of my crew was divided. It made me want to go back to California even sooner. I felt so angry, with all parties involved, and to this day I am angry that I didn't voice how I felt when I had the chance.

I was driving Elaine's car while I was back home visiting. I would pick her up from work, and if I wasn't spending time with Michelle or Michay, then I would spend the night with her. That only happened a couple of times though, considering that I was really there to be with my daughters, I wanted majority of my time to be with them.

I also visited Miya while I was in town. Miya and I use to swing Ep's, while I was messing with Renee and Marie. She told me that she was pregnant when we use to speak on the phone, while I was still in school in Pittsburgh. But she told me that the baby was not mine. She had a man, the whole time that she was messing with me, so I thought maybe it wasn't mine.

Everyone use to joke about how much her son looked like me. I wanted to see for myself, so I went to visit them. Both times that I stopped by to see him, he was not there, but

I was able to see photos. Truthfully, I didn't see the resemblance, and even if there was, I asked Miya several times, and each time I received the words no; so I was through pressing the issue. Deep down inside, I was hoping and praying that he was my son. I just decided to put it in God's hands.

CHAPTER 23
OLD NAVY

After visiting all of my family and friends for a month, I figured that it was time for me to get back to California. Since my altercation at Burger King had left me unemployed, I had to start my job search all over again the minute that I stepped back in town.

The first place that I went to fill out applications was at the Ontario Mills Mall. I applied at several stores, including Old Navy. Dena, who was one of the managers at Old Navy, called me four days later. We set up an interview time date and time for that following Thursday. Dena was the manager that interviewed me, on Thursday and everything went well. She liked the fact that I had a lot of retail experience. She told me that she had a few more people to interview, and then she would be getting back to me.

On Sunday evening, she called me and offered me a seasonal sales position. I needed money to send a little something home to my girls, and to get on with my acting career, so any job was better than none at all.

Once I started working I had a lot of fun. The whole staff was cool, especially this one manager named Andrea. Andrea was short, dark-skinned and real cute. Andrea also didn't take any shit from anybody. I learned immediately that if you wanted to work, there was definitely a job for you here.

The only problem that I had was my scheduling. I was seasonal, so I wasn't in any position to request a custom schedule. It was the holiday season, so I was being scheduled from 6:00 AM till 2:00 PM. My car was still in the shop so transportation was a bit of a problem for me. My aunt took me to work once. She said that it was too early for her to be waking up, so I never asked her again.

I began to wake up at 2:45 AM and leaving the house by 3:15, so that I could get to work by 6:00. I walked about ten to fifteen miles, from Rialto to the Ontario Mills Mall. The first couple of times I was chased half of the way by a Pitbull and a Doberman. Eventually, they caught on to the fact that I walked that way around the same time every morning, so they befriended me. They were no longer barking at me, they would just walk with me. I guess my job was too far for them also, cause they would just stop midway, lie down and just watch me keep going.

Six weeks after I had returned from home, I received a call from Elaine. She told me that she needed to talk to me about something.

"Remember you said that it was ok to have friends?"

Yes, why?

"I never thought that we would speak like we do, once you moved."

So you called me to tell me that you slept with one of your friends?

"You knew. I had told you a long time ago."

No, you never told me. I think I would remember a conversation when a woman that I'm supposed to be with tells me that someone else is hitting the ass.

"Well, we haven't had sex in a while."

What's a while?

"We had a sex a couple of weeks before you came to visit."

You mean to tell me I was there, riding around with you, thinking you were all mine, and the whole time you had been sleeping with someone else. It's a good thing that I kept my proposal to myself.

"You weren't going to propose to me."

Yes, I was. I even looked at rings for the second time in my life. But I am really glad that you told me the truth. If it's not regarding my daughter, please don't call my house again.

Shortly after I started working at Old Navy, they began hiring more people for the holidays. There was this one young lady named Natia. Natia she was nineteen years old, brown and thick with those excuse me hips. You know the kind, that when a woman walks through a crowd all that you hear is excuse me baby, excuse me. Natia looked exactly like Lauren Hill.

One of the things that attracted me to her was the way that she dressed. She didn't dress like she was from Cali. As we began to speak to each other, I found out that she was a print model/Actor who enjoyed traveling, knitting and shopping. That explained why her gear was so diverse, all she did was shop. She would come through in a sweat suit and some kicks one day, then just flip it on you with a real sexy casual outfit, showing all of her curves. She was a real nice and classy young lady.

Natia and I had started to chill together, and we would talk about the entertainment business, relationships, and God. Natia use to go to L.I.F.E. church, but her mother found a new church closer to home. Whenever I wasn't busy we would spend time together, but we were just friends. Natia pushed a black CRV with the darkest limo tint, to keep everything on the DL. She would pick me up from work, every once in a while. I remember one night that she came to pick me up.

I got off at about 10:30 PM. I was walking down the hall towards the exit door with my friends Sharon, buzz and Melvina. As soon as I went out the door Natia was double parked in the parking lot. Sharon went to her window to say what's up and then all I heard was

"Michael somebody's got something for you."

I went over to the passenger side of the truck and opened the door.

Damn baby is it like that?

Natia had on some sexy satin pajamas from Victoria Secrets. She was sitting in driver seat looking good as hell.

"I'm not driving."

She put her leg over on my side of the car and started to move over. I jumped out and went around to the driver side and jumped in. I fastened my seat belt, threw the car in drive and pulled off. Natia turned on the CD Player, and flipped through Kelly Price's CD, stopping at track # 6 Soul of a Woman. I pulled out of the parking lot and drove towards the freeway entrance. Once I got on the freeway Natia said that she had to finish putting her lotion on. She threw her legs up on the dash and started rubbing lotion all over them. I drove into the other lane, looking at those thighs. I got off the freeway, and headed down the street to my house. Natia took off her seatbelt and climbed on top of me.

Aaw Ma you're buggin.

"Just drive, let me worry about everything else."

I continued to look over her shoulder and drive. By the time that I made it home, we had had sex, and she wanted me to come home with her. I was madd tired so I just passed on the idea. I went in the house took a shower and laid in the bed. She called me once she got home and we talked for a while before I went to bed.

The next day we talked early that morning and she said that she would be in LA taking care of some business all day. I got dressed for work early that day, and left the house to catch the bus. I had arrived at the mall early for work that day, so I decided to do a little shopping. As soon as I came out of the first store I saw Natia holding hands with some young kid wit an S Curl in his head. I just laughed and smiled to myself. I stayed behind them the whole time watching them hold hands and kiss each other like two newlyweds. I stayed silent walking just a few paces behind them all the way until I came to Old Navy. I dipped in the store and headed up the side isle all the way to the back of the store.

She called my cell phone a few days later and acted like nothing happened. I was game, so I just played along. We talked for a quick minute, and then she asked me for some money so she could go out with her friends. I told her no, and she started whinning, asking me why.

Were you in the mall on Saturday?

"No, I told you I was going to LA that day."

Oh, Ok.

"Why did you ask me that?"

I was told that you were in the mall, but I figured it wasn't you.

She started yelling and swearing.

Look, I'm going to let you go, cause I see your upset.

[Guilty feet have no rhythm.] She didn't have to lie, we were just friends, but she ended all of that. We stopped speaking after that incident, but I called her about a year later just to say happy birthday. I like to make those out of the blue call's to my old friends; it keeps them reminiscing on the times that were shared between us.

I had received a phone call from Elaine that night also. She had called me to tell me that she was pregnant. She went on and told me that the baby was not mine. That was something different. I liked being on the other side of the fence for a change. For the past few years every time that I heard the words pregnant, it was always followed by and it's yours, so this was kinda cool. She said that she called to tell me that she was pregnant, and to see how I was doing. She also wanted to know when I was coming back to visit. I got my daughter's clothing sizes, so that I could get her a few things from work, and we got off the phone.

CHAPTER 24
AMERICA ONLINE

After my little fling with Natia was over I had really started working out and going to church a little more. My Jetta was out of the shop, so I had means to get around to my auditions now. I continuously read Backstage and The Ross Reports, trying to secure any part whatsoever. I wasn't that successful initially, but I really wasn't hurt by the rejection. My craft wasn't that polished anyway, so receiving no calls in a way saved me a lot of embarrassment. I enrolled myself in a cold reading workshop so that I would be able to market myself better.

In my spare time, when I wasn't at the gym or at work, I would chat on line. I always visited the ebony chat rooms. One day I was browsing around, and I went to the room Ebony& Ivory. That night, I met one of the most wonderful women that God could have ever sent my way. She was a Mexican woman named Annette. Annette was 24 years old at the time and she had a one-year old son named Jordan.

The first thing that she came out and said was that she was not a skinny woman. That didn't bother me anyway, cause I figured that much from the photo that she emailed to me. I immediately let her know that I like my woman at a buck fifty or better anyway. Once we got the weight thing settled, she began telling me more about herself. Annette had just moved back in with her parents, when she got pregnant with Jordan. She had just quit her job in hopes of finding something better.

Annette was always getting dissed by Jordan's father. He had left her for a younger white girl, and she was not too happy about it. I had found out that Mexican's hated loosing their man to a white woman just like the sisters did. He also had never been there to help her with Jordan, so that made matters worse. The fact that she had a baby by a black man, when her parents weren't even aware that she dated blacks, sort of disappointed them. Not so much her mom, but her dad was really in denial. We started to chat all the time and talk about all types of things. I told her all about my three daughters, by three different women, and she never judged me. Even when I told her about my arrest, she still treated me the same.

One week after we had met, we started to talk on the phone. Her voice was just as sweet as her personality. We would spend time talking for hours on the phone.

One day, we decided to meet each other at the movie theater. Once I arrived at the movie theater, I spotted her right away. She was standing by the ticket booth, wearing tight fitting jeans and a Old Navy fleece pullover. I walked up to her and we gave each other a hug. She stopped me as I proceeded to go to the counter to purchase the tickets. She pulled the tickets for the movie out of her pockets. Then she told me that she came to the movie early just to buy them. I asked her to let me pay her back, but she wouldn't take my money. So we both agreed that the next one would be on me. After the movie, I walked her to her truck and we said good night to each other.

Every now and then I would drive over Annette's house to see her and Jordan. She would come out to my car and meet me or, we would meet at the park around the corner. Her father didn't like blacks at all like that, so I wasn't allowed in the house. At first, I didn't care about what her father thought. He was just going to have to get over it and quick too. Annette liked me and I liked her, whether he liked it or not. Jordan was black, and he couldn't change it.

In June of 1998 Annette treated me to a father's day trip to San Diego. We stayed in a nice hotel and walked down by the pier. It was very romantic. Annette was a blessing sent from God himself. Whenever I needed her, she was always there, no questions asked. The only setback to our relationship was that her father didn't approve. That really made her upset at times. All that she wanted was the same as any child; there parent's blessing.

CHAPTER 25
I NEVER TOLD HER THAT I LOVED HER

On July 12, 1998 right after I came into the house from the gym, I received a phone call that would change my life forever. I was up in my room, lying down on the bed when my cousin Quanna asked me to pick up the phone in my room. I picked up the phone and it was my auntie. She was in NY. She had left a few days ago, to be there when my grandmother went to surgery.

What's up auntie?

"Well Brotha, I got some bad news. Mom passed away yesterday."

Aaaw no, not now auntie, don't play like that.

"I'm not and I would never do that. She came out of surgery and she was fine and then she had a seizure."

My heart just stopped and I started to have problems breathing. I just dropped the phone, grabbed my car keys and rushed out of the house. I decided to go for a drive, but I was really starting to have problems breathing so I drove down the street to Arrowhead Medical Center. As soon as I went in, a nurse came out and took my vitals, and listened to my chest. I was pretty bad, because they just took me right in the back and put me on oxygen and gave me a breathing treatment. I felt that my family might be worried because of the way that I left the house, so I asked one of the nurses to call my cousin and let her know that I was in the hospital and that I was ok. I was released from the hospital about four hours later. I got back in my car and drove home. I was really hurt by the fact that my grandmother had passed away, and they told my cousin the day before they told me.

That day we were watching my grandparents 50th Wedding Anniversary on tape, and the whole time that I was watching the film, my grandmother was already gone. My cousin was supposed to tell me, but she felt that it would be too hard for her to do, so she left it up to my aunt. Two weeks prior, I talked to my grandmother about a business that I needed her help with starting and she said my timing was off. I got smart with her and just hung up the phone. I thought that she was just brushing me off. When I left the hospital I realized that she was probably really sick and hurting; that's why the timing wasn't right. I felt so selfish. Another thing that really bothered me was the fact that in all of my 23 years,

I could never recall a time that I told my grandmother that I loved her. I kept remembering the bad things that I had done, like stealing from her purse when I was younger, and disobeying her daily. I felt that I was a poor excuse for a grandchild. I hadn't seen my grandmother in almost two years, and the next time that I would see her would be in a casket.

My cousin and I got on a flight going to NY at 11:00 PM. We arrived the next morning at 7:00 AM. My mother picked me up from the airport, with my daughter Michay, and as soon as I seen her I just broke down. After we got in the car I asked her to take me over my grandfather's house. We pulled up in the yard at my grandfather's house and he was coming out of the back door.

How you doing Pops?

"I'm holding on, how are you?"

I'm hurting Pop's.

"Well you're older and I need you to stay strong for the family."

Ok, I hear you.

Pop's was too strong to shed a tear, but I knew he felt the loss more than any of us did.

I went upstairs for a minute, but I didn't stay long, because it didn't feel right without my Grandmother being there. I told my mother to drop me off on the block, so I could chill wit my crew. I went around the way, and the only one that was out on the block was my man Julian. We kicked it for a minute and I told him the reason why I was back in town. He expressed his sorrow and told me that he would tell everyone that I was back in town. I hopped back in the car and drove up to Mike's to see if Jay was working. As soon as I pulled up he came out and gave me a hug and said that he was sorry about what happened. I chilled at the restaurant for a minute and talked to Jay for a while. About one hour later I went back around the corner to my mom's house. I went to sleep early that night so that I could get up and get ready for the funeral was tomorrow.

The next morning the family met over my grandparent's house. I was not feeling well, and I didn't get any sleep the night before. My stomach was bubbling and I was experiencing increased chest pains.

The pastor said a prayer for the family as we all went to pay our last respects to my grandmother. We all walked into the church and went to the alter to view my grandmother as she laid peacefully in her casket. I hadn't seen my grandmother in two years, and as I continued to walk towards the casket, my legs got weak and I the chest pains were really wearing me down.

I stepped up to the casket and just broke down to my knees. My stomach cramped like never before. I began to ask God why this had to happen to me. Deep down, I knew that she was in a better place, but I was still beating myself up for not visiting her sooner. I hated the fact that I took my grandmother's life for granted. I wanted to just give up on the whole thing and just come back to Buffalo; to hell with all of my dreams and goals.

My aunt helped me to my seat, and it seemed like the minute that I sat down, the casket was closed. The motion was slow moving but the closure was felt throughout my body. It was definitely the end. No more making her mad, just to hear how funny she sounds when she cursed me out, no more pages at 7:41 PM to go play 20 numbers before the machine stops at 7:45. And I will no longer have the chance to tell this woman that molded me into the entrepreneur that I so badly wanted to be that I loved her.

That hurt me the most. I could tell many girls that I dated, just to give them the satisfaction, but here I was 24 years old and I could not ever remember telling my grandmother that I loved her, and now it's too late.

I don't really know what the pastor said during the funeral ceremony, because I was too emotional, so I had to leave the church. I tried to get a hold of myself and view my grandmother's body one last time as she lay in the casket; before being driven out to her out to her final resting place. But I experienced the same stomach cramps and I could no longer hold the tears back.

At the burial site, I waited back away from the family, until the ceremony was over and she was lowered into the ground, before I approached her casket and had my last conversation with one of the greatest women that I have ever met.

Mom the argument that we had a few weeks prior to this, I'm sorry for being selfish.

And all the times that I caused you hurt and pain, I'm sorry.

For the many times when you wanted to talk to me on the phone and I just rushed you off, I would do anything to have that conversation now.

For the times that you wanted me to stop by and I put my friends and the streets before you, I'm sorry.

And Momma for all of these twenty-five years, that I never told you that I loved you, I'm sorry.

I love you Mom and I will never forget you and everything that you have done for me. I love you with all of my heart and I always will.

I left the cemetery and we went back to the church to join the rest of the family for dinner. I didn't have much of an appetite, so I passed on a dinner plate. I was ready to leave, and I wanted to get as far away as possible. I got dressed and went on the block. As soon as I got out the car, and sat down on the porch, he knew that I needed to be alone.

"Mike take the bike and just come back in a few hours."

Baby had a 1996 Suzuki Katana that was blue and yellow. I strapped on the helmet, hopped on the bike and smashed out. I rushed down the city streets, looking death in it's eyes, traveling at speeds up to 100 mph. I got on the 33 Expressway, put the bike in fifth gear and race down road, thinking about my life, my choices, and my chances. As I was approaching a freeway exit, I came to a stop. I pulled into the parking lot and just sat there for a minute and questioned God about my destiny, purpose, and ultimate position in life.

I didn't receive an answer to that question, cause it was something that I already knew. I was here on earth to Act. To perform and persuade, to build, not destroy, to teach after I have successfully learned and to truly enjoy life, only after I have learned to love.

I don't know what I would have done without Baby being there for me. Baby was Boogie's older brother, he was always cool, but this trip made us closer. We talked like never before, and he expressed interest in things that I was unaware was of any interest o him.

He kept me busy, cause he knew that I was not happy being there. He understood the pain that I felt and he expressed it in many ways, the bike loan was just one. God uses people in many different ways. I truly believe that Baby was my Guardian Angel, there to watch out for me and to make sure that I made it back to California.

CHAPTER 26
MOESHA

One week later, I went back to Cali. I wrote in my Journal, the whole time that I was on the plane. That was something that I haven't done in a while. I had spoken to Annette a few days earlier, and she agreed to pick me up from the airport. As soon as I got off the plane, she was waiting there to greet me. That is one of the warmest feelings in the world; Someone greeting you when your plane arrives. We greeted each other with a hug then we went to get my bags. We stopped off at the West Covina Mall, where I took advantage of a sale at Macy's, then she dropped me off at home.

I called Andrea as soon as I came into town from Annette's cell-phone. Andrea was one of the manager's at Old Navy, and I just wanted to let her know that I was back and available for work. I went back to work, but I wasn't the same joking person that I was prior to my trip back home. My attitude was rude and I no longer wanted all the responsibility that I had been given previously. I felt that I was overworked and underpaid. I also felt that my job was becoming a drain on me. I had become content with Old Navy, and that is not what I came to Cali for. Something had to be done.

In November of 1998 I moved into my own apartment in San Bernardino, CA. Annette helped me move in and she bought little nick nacks for the place also. Her and Jordan would come over for a while, but her parents would always page her and tell her to come home. Being with Annette was like pulling teeth. Everything would be smooth, and then a phone-call would ruin everything.

I started mailing my photo's and resumes to agents and casting directors. I had to get focused on my career and goals. I had not been putting forth the effort that I had initially, when I first moved out here.

After I moved it became very impossible for our relationship to grow. The more time that we spent, the more we would grow apart. I was growing real tired of her parents, not letting her live her life. I was getting tired of being judged by her parents. Annette wanted a relationship that would possibly grow into a marriage proposal. She knew that she was not going to get that from me, cause I told her when we first met that I was in California to focus on my career.

One day in December, while I was at work, my pager went off. I looked down to read the numbers, but I was unable to, cause the caller left a voicemail. I was working at the registers at the time, and there was a line, so I would have to check it later.

When I finally was able to take my break, I went into the manager's office to see if I could make an emergency phone call. When I called my voice mail, as soon as I entered my code there was a young lady named faye with a message as follows.

"My name is Faye, and I'm currently casting for Moesha, to work on tomorrow's show. If you get this message before 7:00 PM please give me a call back. I will be in the office late this evening."

I hung up the phone and immediately called her back. When she answered I introduced myself and told her that I was still at work. I asked her if I could call her back when I made it home in about 45 minutes. She agreed, and we hung up with each other.

I left work a few minutes later and as soon as I stepped in to my apartment door I returned her call. The phone was answered on the second ring.

"Monica Cooper Casting, this is Faye speaking."

Hello Faye this is Michael Martin returning your call.

"Oh, yes Michael, I came across your picture and I was wondering if you're available to do some work on Moesha tomorrow morning?"

Yes, I'm available to work tomorrow.

"Great your call time is 10:00 AM, you must be on time. Also Michael I need you to bring with you two changes of clothing. Bring one sporty outfit and another that's more casual."

Ok.

"You are to report to the Sunset and Gower Studios on Melrose Ave."

Ok, Faye, I have all of the information written down and I will be there at 10 O' clock sharp.

I hung up the phone, and ran around my apartment. Then I just stopped and dropped to my knees and thanked God. I didn't mail any photos to Faye, and she just called me out of the blue and said that she came across my photo. There is only one person who made it possible for Faye to receive that photo, and that was the lord above. I sat on my knees and just thanked God out loud for almost 10 minutes. Then I called my mother followed by Annette to tell them the good news.

I had to travel from San Bernardino to Hollywood, on the world famous 10 fwy. The next morning I left my house at 7:30 AM. Traffic was running smooth until I came upon the 405 interchange. The freeway is always congested around there. By the time that I made it down to the 101 fwy, it was 9:55 PM. I was pissed. This was not the first impression that I had in mind.

I finally made it to the gate at the studio. The security checked my name off the list and issued me a pass. I hurried up and parked my car and grabbed my things. I was headed around towards the dressing room, when another gentleman told me that I was headed in the wrong direction and that I was late. When I stepped into the dressing room, it was packed with actors to the point where I could not move. The casting director came in behind me and started to take roll. She was followed by the set director who immediately pointed me out and said you're going to be my dancer # 1. He assigned two other gentlemen to be dancers # 2 and # 3. He left the room and said that he would be back to get us in a minute. One of the other dancers said,

"You're the man, have you worked the show before?"

No, this is my first time, but why do you say that?

"Because you're #1, that means that you get to dance with Brandy."

I didn't want to make myself seem like a groupie or unprofessional, but I was siked. I was happy all in the inside. I guess this was the big payback, from all of those times that Jay and I drove around Bumping Brandy's first LP. Me and Jay put her first CD on the map in Buffalo.

The wardrobe personnel came up to our dressing room to check everyone's wardrobe. At the time I was rocking MY Girbaud Jeans, a gold Eddie Bauer sweater, my gold timbs, and my cream and gold Avirex jacket. She told me that my outfit was perfect, but I couldn't wear the jacket because of the advertisement factors.

At about 12 noon, all of the actors had arrived. We all went downstairs and took our positions. For the rehearsal they have a stand in for Brandy, and a few of the other actors, so we all just go through the scenes improvising.

The set director then told me what I was supposed to do.

"Brandy is the girl you've been eyeing in the club. I want you to bogard your way through the crowd, grab her hand and lead her to the dance floor. The two of you should dance until you hear cut."

Ok, let's do it.

We tried it a few times and I made a few mistakes the first couple of times, but then I was ready for them to bring out Brandy. We went through all of the scene's and by the time that we were done it was time to eat lunch. All of the actors except the stars ate in the kitchen eating area that is located right there on the same lot.

The food was decent and the desert was on time. As soon as we were done, eating all of the actors had to get dressed. While we were eating, the studio audience was being seated, and we go through the whole episode with them present. We were able to leave after we had completed all of our scenes.

I was on point and I pushed up on Brandy strong as hell. She came off the couch and we were dancing like we were on Soul Train. We cut and they went to the next scene. I had to rush to the dressing room, to get ready for my second scene.

As soon as I came back down the stairs they were calling for places everyone. We did that scene, and after that I was free to go. I left the studio that night at 8:30 PM. As soon as I was done, I hopped right on the freeway, and drove straight home.

My entire time driving home all that I could do was continue to thank God. I had been through the storm, and I finally made it to the other side. I had focused on God first and my career second. I was now beginning to reap the benefits that I had spent so many nights praying for. I knew that I had to continue to stay on the right path, and always put God first. I came from Buffalo, and never thought that I would get out, and here I was just one year later, dancing with Brandy in front of millions, and all of my hard work and the struggles really paid off. I was able to turn all the negative statements that people said about me and use them to fuel my success.

I didn't make millions for my appearance, but considering what I've been through; I felt like a million dollars on the inside and that's all that mattered to me. I was finally taking charge of my destiny. The last thing that I asked God was, how long were all of these blessing going to last? I found out very soon that my hopes and dreams would be shattered once again.

THE END